EXECUTION OF FAITH

STEPHEN TAYLOR

STEPHEN TAYLORBOOKS

www.dissectdesigns.com

Copyright © 2018 Stephen Taylor
All rights reserved.
ISBN: 978-1-7391636-1-7

DANNY PEARSON WILL RETURN

For updates about current and upcoming releases, as well as exclusive promotions, visit the authors website at:

www.stephentaylorbooks.com

ALSO BY STEPHEN TAYLOR
THE DANNY PEARSON THRILLER SERIES

Snipe

Heavy Traffic

The Timekeepers Box

The Book Signing

Vodka Over London Ice

Execution Of Faith

Who Holds The Power

Alive Until I Die

Sport of Kings

Blood Runs Deep

Command To Kill

No Upper Limit

Leave Nothing To Chance

CHAPTER 1

'**M**orning, Nigel. Where's the prince? Still in bed?' said Danny Pearson to his security colleague Nigel as he entered the penthouse suite of the Hyatt Regency in Dubai.

'No, no, he's having a swim up top. Says he's going to attend the plastic pollution seminar this morning,' Nigel replied.

Both men raised their eyebrows.

'Anything else.'

'Nah, oh, apart from we gotta new guy making up the rooms.'

The hairs on the back of Danny's neck stood up as he moved quickly into the master bedroom. Spying the abandoned cleaning trolley triggered images of the maid he'd passed in the corridor looking for her cleaning kit. From the top of the stairs he heard the faint click of the rooftop terrace door shutting.

'Nigel, on me. Cody, get your arse up to the terrace *now*,' shouted Danny through the radio, already halfway up the stairs.

Reaching the door he stopped, allowing himself a second to assess the situation. He hoped he'd got it wrong. The prince was climbing out of the far end of the pool, unaware of the young Arabic man in the hotel uniform walking towards him, a towel by his side, one corner held awkwardly.

Danny opened the door and slipped through, with Nigel behind him. He heard movement at the bottom of the stairs as Cody entered the apartment. Danny walked forward on his toes, silently. The man was unaware of their presence, his focus fixed firmly on the prince.

Cody burst through the terrace door like a bull in a china shop. Everyone froze, then looked at each other. The man's eyes went wide with fear before narrowing with determination. Dropping the towel, he exposed a three-foot curved Arabian sword glinting in the sun light.

The scene went from still to crazy in a blink of the eye. The man raised the sword and ran screaming in Arabic at the horrified prince. Danny powered after him trying to catch up. Not fast enough. There was only one course of action. As the attacker rounded the corner of the pool he used a sun lounger like a trampoline and launched himself into a dive, body-tackling the swordsman just a few feet short of the prince.

They crashed into the sofas and coffee table by the pool. The small, lean swordsman scrambled to his feet swinging wildly with the razor-sharp blade. Danny instinctively pulled one of the seat cushions in front of himself. The razor sharp blade almost cut it in two, its silver tip halting only inches from his nose. Danny shot upright as the sword drew back, adrenaline pumping through his veins as if charged with electricity. Jumping back in time to avoid the swishes of a double attack. Grabbing the corner of a towel off the seat beside him, Danny whipped it quickly at the glinting blade as it sliced its way towards him. The towel spun around the sword, catching tightly on itself as it went. Using his power and weight advantage, he wrenched hard. The sword flew from the attacker's grip and plopped into the pool behind him.

The swordsman stood stunned as Danny threw his full weight into a punch. The attacker's nose moved one way and his head the other. The blow sent the little man flying backwards over the sofa. Nigel and Cody dived to apprehend him. They needn't have bothered—he was flat on his back, out cold.

Shaking his bruised fist, Danny turned to check on the prince. He'd expected the man to look shocked and shaken but His Royal Pain in the Arse was grinning from ear to ear, jumping up and down and cheering.

Two days. Just two more days and I go home.

CHAPTER 2

The neglected six-storey apartment building stood on one of the less desirable streets in Greenwich Village, New York. A rusted fire escape zigzagged its way down the front between windows peeling with old black paint. The communal entrance door was scratched and worn around the lock through which residents had stabbed their keys a million times over the years. Twenty-four buzzers sat on the wall beside it. Most were covered with tape or labels on top of labels that hid an ever-changing history of occupants. In his one-bedroom rented apartment, Bradley White rifled through a pile of dirty washing until he found an old sweatshirt. It passed the sniff test—just. He'd worked night and day for the past two weeks and his domestic duties had been rather neglected. There were no clean clothes and the kitchen sink was besieged by a large, teetering pile of crusty cups, plates and cutlery. The whole lot stunk. Undeterred Bradley generously sprayed himself and the sweatshirt with deodorant, and pulled the garment over his head, onto his skinny torso through a cloudy aerosol haze. He checked his emails on his computer while brushing his greasy hair. His eyes lit up as a CMS payment email pinged into view.

'Shit! Oh, yes!'

He jumped up and hunted for his phone, eventually finding it wrapped up in his bunched duvet. Logging onto his banking app he waited. After a few tense seconds, $3135 displayed on the monitor.

'Yes!'

He thumped down on the beaten-up old sofa, bought from a garage sale around the corner. Letting out a big sigh, he gazed up at the damp patch in the corner. The mould was creeping its slimy way down from the ceiling to the wall.

Ive gotta get out of this shithole.

Leaping up he grabbed his keys and wallet, then slammed the door as he left the apartment.

It was a warm spring morning, and the short walk lifted his mood. He was starting to feel positive about his future prospects.

He grabbed a seat outside his favourite coffee shop in the heart of the Village. This was the trendy part of town, he went there two or three times a week pretending it was because he liked it so much. In reality, it was because he fancied the waitress and was trying to work up enough courage to ask her out. Sitting nervously as she came over he managed to stutter his order, a lump in his throat ending further conversation. He sipped his latte and munched on a frosted doughnut, taking peeks at the waitress from the corner of his eye as she served drinks and cleared tables.

The phone vibrated in his pocket. He took it out and looked at the caller ID.

Shit.

'Err, hello?'

5

'Bradley, it's Marcus. I've just been going over your program submission. Excellent work. We are most pleased.'

'Okay, th-thank you.'

'I trust you have upheld the confidentiality agreement,' said Marcus. His English impeccable, his tone devoid of emotion.

'Yeah, I mean of course. There's nothing other than the copy I sent you and the working copy on my computer,' said Bradley quick to please Marcus.

'Excellent. I'll be in New York next week on business. We will meet then and discuss your future with CMS. Oh, and pay your completion bonus, of course.'

'Yes, great. Thank you, Mr Tenby. I look for—'

Marcus had already hung up. Still, yes! At last, the break he'd been waiting for. Now he could move out of his shithole apartment and get something more in-keeping with his up-and-coming status. Yep, this was a great day.

Finishing his doughnut he picked up his coffee cup, then strolled off down a quiet side street with a spring in his step. He headed towards Fifth Avenue and Washington Square. As he passed Kremer Property Lettings, Bradley paused to browse the window displays. Pictures of modern uptown apartments he'd previously only dreamed of now leaped out at him. He continued walking, daydreaming of a posh new apartment, then turned his thoughts to the lure of an immediate shopping spree.

As he crossed an intersection, someone called him. He paused halfway.

'Hey, Bradley, over here.'

Turning to look, his eyes searching the other side of the street for the source of the voice. It came from a service bay opposite. Large refuse bins lined up neatly along its rear. In a doorway to one side, a figure in blue workwear and a baseball cap waved at him.

6

'Sorry, do I know—'

His legs buckled from under him. The sound of bones breaking below the knee vibrated sickeningly through his body. Time froze in his mind's eye like a sports playback, delaying the massive impact on his lower back milliseconds later. His head and shoulders whipped back and struck a hard, metallic surface, as it reverberated to his core. The delivery truck hit Bradley hard from behind. Its bumper shattered his legs before his lower back made contact with the curved front. He stared at the blue sky above as his head and shoulders were forced backwards, planting him firmly onto of the sloping metal surface of the hood. With his head tilted upwards in a paralysed gaze, he was carried across the street into the service bay. The truck plowed into the refuse bins lining the dead end wall, the metal sides of one bending around Bradley's body as the truck crunched to a stop. He coughed up a fountain of blood through his mouth as his internal organs were crushed.

In the seconds before consciousness left him and the life seeped out of his broken body, Bradley looked at his hand and blinked. It was settled, as if purposely, on top of the refuse bin, the coffee cup sitting neatly upright.

This isn't right. My job, my money, my apartment...

CHAPTER 3

The driver was out of the cab with surprising speed given his stature—a thick, solid neck and arms like tree trunks. He was dressed in a plain navy-blue uniform with a peaked baseball cap pulled low down to meet his wrap-around shades. He wore heavy rubber gloves; the kind used by manual workers when moving crates or building blocks around. His accomplice opened the passenger door and stepped towards the seat.

'Fifteen seconds, Snipe.'

Snipe leaned in, flashing him a look. 'Yeah, yeah. You ready? On three.'

Peters undid the seatbelt holding the passenger in place—a wretched skinny man with filthy jeans and a stinking sweatshirt. They pulled his sleeves up to the elbows, exposing scabbed, needle-marked flesh. Tape across his left arm held a syringe firmly in position so it wouldn't come out. A baseball cap pulled down low covered his head as it slumped forward his chin on his chest. He was alive but not conscious.

'One, two, three,' Peters said, as they slid the man

8

across to the driver's seat. Snipe removed the cap, revealing a smashed-up, bloody nose and knocked-out front teeth. He grabbed the back of the man's head with his massive hand and smashed his face into the steering wheel. Peters pressed down on the syringe plunger in the junkie's arm then removed it and put it in his pocket. As he backed out and shut the cab door, he looked down at the side of the truck, then moved to the buckled front.

'Thirty seconds,' Peters said, looking at his watch. 'Get his phone. And don't tread in the blood. I don't want any footprints. Hurry up,' he continued, his voice low and controlled.

The junkie in the driver's seat convulsed and opened his eyes for just a fleeting second before they rolled back in his head. The massive heroin overdose stopping his miserable heart.

Waiting at the door to the building, Peters looked through the small gap between the truck and service bay wall. Witnesses on the street had been screaming and shouting, but the initial shock was starting to fade, and people were tentatively approached the rear of the truck.

'Fuck's sake, hurry up, Snipe. Forty seconds.'

Snipe swung himself over the broken heap of Bradley's body.

'Got it,' he said, grinning as he flew past Peters, who pulled the door shut behind them sliding the deadbolt into place. With the door locked, they disappeared deep into the empty building. Moments later they surfaced casually from a door on the street around the corner. The police report would be brief. A known drug addict steals a truck, passes out while overdosing, killing a young man before crashing into a service bay. Both men found dead on arrival.

A white Amos Electrical Goods van sat waiting for

Snipe and Peters as they exited the building. Snipe climbed into the back, the van rocking to one side with his weight as he did so. He sat down next to a lean, pointy-faced man with small round glasses and slicked-back ginger hair. The guy looked out of place in his navy work clothes; too neat, more intellectual, like an IT consultant or a banker. A suit and briefcase would have suited him better.

'All good, mate?' he said with a strong, upbeat Australian accent.

'No sweat, Smithy. Like a dream. Peters was doing his fucking clock-watching again—ten seconds, twenty seconds, blah fucking blah,' said Snipe.

His voice was thick and gravelly, betraying his London roots. A Cheshire-cat grin filled his face, though his eyes kept their usual lack of emotion—ice-cold blue orbs that cut right through you.

With his huge muscular body and thick neck, Snipe was massive compared to Smith. He took off his cap to reveal a short blond crewcut. There was an underlying menace about him, like a firework just about to go off.

Peters got in the front passenger seat. He didn't look at anyone in the van, just scanned the sidewalk. Cold eyes, so dark you couldn't tell the iris from the pupil, darted around as he assessed his surroundings. Lifting his cap he ran his fingers through his wavy brown hair that greyed at the sides. Pulling his cap back into place, he turned to the driver.

'Take us to his apartment, Rami. Nice and slow. Keep to the speed limits. Should be five and half minutes,' Peters said to the stocky Mexican.

Five and a half minutes. Here he goes again.

'Wanker,' muttered Snipe.

The van pulled gently out into the flow of traffic as the police and ambulance sirens echoed their imminent arrival.

Exactly five and a half minutes later, Bradley's run-down apartment block came into view. The Amos van pulled up into a space two cars down from the communal entrance door. Peters' mobile vibrated with an incoming message.

He glanced down for a couple of seconds then scanned the sidewalk and checked his watch.

'I want to be in and out within fifteen minutes.'

They checked that the cuffs and collars of their uniforms were buttoned up and pulled on new latex gloves. Snipe and Smith got out of the van and pulled the peaks of their caps low. Walking around to the back they opened the rear doors.

In the front, Peters took hold of a clipboard and Ramirez grabbed a small tool bag. After one final look around they hopped out of the van. Scanning the street in both directions they walked casually towards the apartment block's entrance. At the door, Ramirez dropped to his knees while Peters stood in front of him, facing the van to mask him from view.

At the van Snipe and Smith unloaded a large-boxed washing machine onto an orange sack barrow. Peters heard the faint click of the lock behind him and gave an almost imperceptible nod to Snipe.

Ramirez jammed a screwdriver under the door to hold it in place then entered the foyer and headed straight up the stairs, Peters followed him in tapping the lift-call button before going up the stairs.

'Two minutes,' he said.

As the bell rang to announce the lift's arrival, Snipe's huge bulk wheeled the washing machine through the entrance. Smith followed removing the screwdriver, letting the door shut behind them.

Up on the third floor, Ramirez crouched by Bradley's apartment door while Peters took lookout, his eyes darting between the lift and the stairs above and below.

As the lift door opened, Peters heard a soft click behind him. Ramirez was in.

'Three minutes thirty,' Peters said as he stepped forward, allowing Snipe and Smithy to wheel the washing machine inside.

Snipe turned his head, he was about to mutter something, but Peters shot him a steely look and he thought better of it.

Peters took one last look then entered the apartment—the last in. He gently clicked the door shut behind him. Snipe lifted the lid off the washing machine box to reveal an empty crate.

Lifting the paper on his clipboard Peters read out the list of instructions.

'Ramirez—take the bedroom. Snipe—get all computer equipment from the lounge and dust the desk afterwards so you can't see what we've taken. Smith—kitchen. I'll get any paperwork in here. In the box and out the door in ten minutes, gentlemen. We've got to destroy this lot and ditch the van by twelve. Our flight leaves at 4.00 p.m.'

Snipe grabbed two of the four wipe-down cloths in the bottom of the crate and threw one to Smith before moving off towards the computer desk.

'Dust the desk? This place is such a shithole it'll be the only clean spot in it,' he muttered, resisting the temptation to hurl the computer at Peters.

He unplugged the monitor, mouse and keyboard and packed them into the crate.

'Ten minutes, gentlemen,' Snipe mimicked. 'Fucking wanker.'

UNTITLED

4

Tired and hungry after a long flight, Danny strolled out of passport control and into the arrivals hall of London Heathrow's Terminal 5. It was 8.00 p.m. and dark outside. The harsh artificial light of the terminal building sucked the colour out of everything, giving its travellers an unhealthy, jaundiced look. He crossed the shiny, polished floor and exited into the chilly London drizzle. Carrying nothing but his frayed old army backpack, he made for the taxi rank.

'Home sweet home.'

In jeans, a T-shirt and just a light canvas jacket, he contemplated his poor choice of clothes. Even so after four months in the heat of Dubai, the chilly drizzle of his home city was strangely comforting.

His pocket vibrated with the steady rhythm of an incoming call. Fished the phone from his jacket pocket he smiled as he looked at the illuminated screen.

'Yo, little bruv, I'm just about to get a taxi to yours,' he said.

'Nah, don't do that. I told Scott you were coming home. He's driven me down to pick you up. We're a few minutes away. Look out for a blue BMW M4.' Rob's voice shrieked over loud music and the powerful car's throaty exhaust.

Swinging around on his heels Danny headed back towards the pickup point.

'He always was a flash bastard. See you in a minute,' he said flicking the phone off and shoving it back into his soggy jacket pocket.

He'd known Scott Miller nearly all his life, from way back at primary school. They'd gone in very different directions over the years but remained steadfast friends.

Scott was a computer genius and recently divorced. Although his ex-wife had cost him the marital home and a small fortune, he still seemed to have more than his fair share of spare cash. He lived in a swanky new apartment that overlooked the Thames and it seemed he'd ditched the Porsche for a BMW.

This confirmed Danny's theory that Scott, although only thirty-four, was in the middle of an early mid-life crisis. All he needed was a young, skinny super model on his arm and the picture would be complete.

As the gurgling BMW pulled into the pickup zone. A grinning Rob climbed out and the two brothers gave each other a quick hug and a slap on the back.

'Get a room, you tarts,' said Scott with his nasally aristocratic voice.

Swinging his head down to look at Scott, Danny said. 'Nice to see you too, you posh prick.'

Rob climbed into the back while Danny dumped his bag in the boot and took the front seat. Before he'd could click his seatbelt in place, Scott had gunned the car out onto the exit road.

'Four months in Dubai and you haven't even got a suntan, old chap,' said Scott grinning.

'I've spent the past four months standing in a hallway, waiting for His Royal pain in the arse to sober up and get out of bed,' Danny chuckled, electing not to reveal his near miss with a sword-wielding lunatic.

'Paul really stitched you up on that one, bruv,' said Rob.

Scott pulled onto the M4, heading towards central London.

'Nah, Paul was short on guys and I owed him a favour. I knew it would be a boring gig before I went. Paid bloody well, though.' Danny glanced around out of the window.

'Where are we going, Scotty? I thought we were going to Rob's.'

'Change of plan, old man. You're all stopping at mine tonight. We could go to yours, I suppose, but wait—you haven't got anywhere, have you?' Scott said, grinning.

Danny threw him a steely look. 'You do know how easily I could kill you, don't you, Scott?' he said before cracking a wide grin.

'The way he drives, you won't need to,' said Rob pipin, up from the back.

'When you ladies have quite finished, what do you want to eat? Chinese, pizza or Indian?'

'Chinese!' Rob shouted.

Danny shrugged. 'I'm easy—whatever you guys want.'

Scott put his foot down and moved into the right-hand lane. 'Chinese it is then,' he said before changed his tone. 'I need to have a serious chat with you later,' he said.

Puzzled, Danny looked at him and frowned. 'That sounds ominous, Scotty boy.'

'It might be, old chap. It just might be.'

Loaded with beer and Chinese food, they sat in front of the enormous TV screen that hung on the living-room wall. A football match blared out of the room's surround-sound through huge Bang & Olufsen speakers.

Scott sat in a big, comfy leather recliner. He was slim and athletic with a year-round tan the same colour as the chair leather. His floppy, sand-coloured hair bounced up and down as he laughed and joked with the two brothers. He had the smooth, rich British toff look down to a tee.

Danny sunk into the sofa like a polar opposite. Six foot two and seventeen stone of solid muscle that flexed periodically through his t-shirt, even though his face was warm and cheerful as they talked. His brother and lifelong friend knew only too well how it could turn granite hard and dangerous. His deep-brown eyes burned intensely—always alert, always assessing, even when relaxed. Years of SAS service and training had left him with ingrained heightened awareness.

Rob was a softer, smaller, and younger version of Danny. They looked like brothers but Rob's career as a graphic designer had given him a pasty office look. His shoulders were slightly hunched from hours bent over a computer and his stomach was showing the beginnings of a belly.

'Love the new pad, Scott,' Danny said. 'What's one of these set you back, mate?'

'Oh about a one and a half million,' Scott said.

'Shit, how the hell did you get so rich tapping a keyboard all day?'

'Because I'm the mutt's nuts, old chap. And that reminds me—I need your advice on something.'

'Fire away,' Danny said, glancing at his brother snoring happily in one of the recliners.

'Do you remember that pretty little thing from Japan a few years ago—Amaya Sato? She was over here on a university internship and worked for me on the software contract for HSBC,' said Scott.

Danny could hear a slight sadness in his voice.

'You mean the one your ex-wife found you in bed with?' he said, grinning.

'Err, yes,' said Scott.

'Anyway, we put that all that behind us. And apart from that, she was an exceptional programmer,' he said regaining his composure. 'She's been working on a software project for a private firm and is rather worried about the client's credibility. She's discovered hidden spyware on the computer they supplied. Sophisticated stuff—cloaked open-mic channels, constantly streaming webcam feeds, hidden remote access... all that sort of thing,' said Scott wandering over to the fridge to get another beer.

'She's pretty worried. Even contacted me from a cyber cafe to make sure no one monitored her. She sent me a copy of the program and asked if I could check it out for her,' he finished taking a big gulp from his can.

Danny shrugged. 'If she's finished the program, isn't it a bit irrelevant, mate? Job done, surely.'

'No, old chap. She told them she's a month away from finishing. Gives me time to have a look.'

'Come on, Scotty. I don't get it. What's the big deal? You're the whizz-kid.'

'Okay, okay. I'm getting to it. Amaya's written a beast of a program to a given specification. It's part of an access program for the banking industry—nothing strange there. Problem is the way they asked her to design it. It's weird. It's a full program in its own right, but designed to be part

17

of additional links. Very sophisticated, and on its own not too interesting. But the links are masked and allow access from remote programs. You could potentially access and cripple or control the entire system her program is on. Probably a bit cloak and dagger, I know, but still strange enough to warrant checking it out, don't you think?' asked Scott taking another swig of his beer.

'I've got some company information and a name. Marcus Tenby. The company's here in London. CMS Software Corporation.'

'Again, you're the whizz-kid. What's this got to do with me?'

'I was thinking you could run it by Paul. He must still have contacts interested in this sort of thing. You know, favours to call in and all that.'

'I guess so. I can give him a call tomorrow, but no promises. It sounds a bit far-fetched to me,' said Danny stretching and yawning.

'Do us a favour—wake up dozy bollocks over there and send him to bed. I'm beat, mate. Going to turn in.'

CHAPTER 4

The old Land Cruiser bounced and shook its occupants violently as it hurtled across the barren landscape. Rufus Petrov was wedged between two black-clad soldiers wielding AK-47 rifles. A former major in the KGB, he was as corrupt today as he'd been back then. Despite their best efforts, the young extremists in the car didn't intimidate him. Nor was he bothered by the heat and discomfort from the hours of bone-crunching along Syria's dirt-track roads.

He had a meeting with General Akbar Bakr, leader of an Islamic extremist group calling themselves The Faith. Tucked safely in his rucksack was a vacuum-sealed container that Akbar wanted desperately.

It had been twelve hours since his guide led him undetected across the Turkish border. Before being driven by his escorts in a zigzag route to avoid Kurdish freedom fighters.

Finally the encampment came into view with its high perimeter wall and armed guards. They stopped at the entrance barrier with its 50-calibre Browning M2 machine gun pointing at them from behind its sandbagged bunker. The guards waved them through. Their arrival sparking much excitement and hollering. Petrov looked blankly on. Secretly he despised these amateurs—brainwashed screaming idiots, pawns intimidated by leaders who sent them to their deaths in the name of a religion they didn't even believe in. Like the tyrants before them, it was all about power and money. The car pulled to a stop in the middle of a yard surrounded by single-storey whitewashed buildings, presumably a mixture of barracks, armoury, cells and officers quarters. Stepping out of the car he watched as five men in headscarves and long white robes walked briskly across the dusty yard towards him. The man at the front smiling warmly as he extended his hand.

'Mr Petrov, I am Akbar Bakr. Welcome, welcome. Come. Let me get you some refreshment,' said Bakr beckoning him towards one of the whitewashed buildings.

The walls were thick and the interior cool. Petrov shook the other four leaders hands before taking a seat on one of the many large cushions scattered around the floor.

'Tea, Mr Petrov?' said Bakr.

'Yes, thank you.'

A young boy scooted in nervously to serve the refreshments. He stumbled slightly in front of Petrov, spilling a few drops tea on his leg as the cup changed hands. Akbar shouted furiously at the cowering boy, then smacked him around the head before kicking him out the door.

Regaining his composure, Bakr returned to his seat. 'My apologies.'

'It is nothing. Do not worry. Shall we get down to business, Mr Bakr?'

'Of course. You have the sample with you?'

Petrov opened his rucksack and pulled out the silver container. It looked like a small Thermos flask.

'Do you have the room set up for the demonstration?' he said.

'Yes. If you would like to follow me.' Bakr led him outside and into the building next door.

The space was large and square. In its centre stood a sealed, plastic, blow-up chemical-incident tent with a double-entry door centre stage. Inside the bubble sat a heavy chair with shackles attached to it's arms and legs.

'American military. Best quality,' said Bakr, smiling proudly.

'Is it airtight?' said Petrov curtly.

'Of course. We are not amateurs,' snapped Bakr. He turned to his next-in-command. 'Hani, go get the boy.'

An uneasy silence followed until Hani appeared, pushing the wide-eyed boy who'd served the tea in front of him. The boy tried to pull away when he saw the tent, but his small, thin frame was no match for the two grown men. They dragged him through the airlock and pushed him roughly down into the chair.

'No, please. Let me go. Please!' he begged, tears streaming down his face.

Container in hand, Petrov approached the plastic siding. There was a zipped access point to a boxed section inside the tent. He twisted the lid, which came away with a hiss. Inside the container, surrounded by heavy padding, was a tiny compressed canister with a protective cap on top. Unzipping the boxed section, Petrov placed the canister inside and resealed it. He glanced at the whimpering boy, whose wide eyes followed his ever move, and slid his arms into two long gloves attached to the siding of the tent. Opening the little airlock seal between the tent and the box, he removed the canister pulling off the cap. While staring stony-eyed at the boy, he pressed the release button. A small cloud of vapour drifted up from the canister before dissipating. Petrov dropped the canister and pulled his arms out of the gloves, before standing back to allow the others to see.

Bakr and his men stepped forward and watched intently. For thirty seconds, nothing happened. Then the boy inhaled deeply and started coughing and wheezing as he pulled at his restraints. His small frame convulsed as Bakr's eyes gleamed, a wide grin spread across his face. Blood streamed from the boy's nose followed by his tear ducts. He shook violently while his eyes pleaded with them, finally coughing and spewing blood from his mouth. His body spasmed one final time before he went into cardiac arrest.

'Excellent,' said Bakr, patting Petrov on the back.

'The nerve agent is active for forty-eight hours once airborne. After that, you need to suck the air out through the chemical-wash filter. Then dig a big hole and burn the tent with the boy still inside it. Use plenty of fuel,' Petrov said, a hint of boredom in his voice.

'And you can get the consignment to London as agreed?' said Bakr leading the Russian out of the room.

'As long as I receive the payment as agreed, you will receive the consignment,' replied Petrov.

'Payment will be with you tomorrow, my friend.' They sat back down on the plump cushions. 'More tea before we escort you back across the Turkish border?' He clapped his hands.

'Thank you,' said Petrov as Hani dragged another nervous young boy through the door.

CHAPTER 5

Rolling over in bed Danny picked up his trusty old G-Shock watch. He groaned as 4.45 a.m. stared back at him.

Heads still on Dubai time.

He spent another half-hour trying to convince himself he'd go back to sleep, before giving up and getting out of bed. Turning the lamp on he rummaged around in his old army backpack until he found a crumpled t-shirt and running shorts.

Time to clear his head.

Grabbing a bottle of water from the fridge, he picked up Scott's electronic fob so he could get back into the building without disturbing the others. Clicking the apartment door softly closed behind him. He ignored the lift and took the stairs to the ground floor foyer. The building had only recently been completed and still smelled of new paint and vinyl. Once outside he looked up at the contemporary building and smiled. All grey panels and glass windows.

A million five? Really?

After a quick stretch he broke into a brisk run along the footpath that followed the bank of the Thames towards the city centre. The tall buildings of Canary Wharf were silhouetted in the distance as the first light of dawn crept across London. At quiet times like these, painful memories of Sarah and Timmy snuck in, engulfing him in a deep sadness and overwhelming loneliness. Seven years had passed since his wife and son were killed in a hit-and-run, but it was though it were yesterday. He'd blamed himself for not being there to protect them. Instead, he'd been on tour thousands of miles away, saving lives for a country that didn't give a shit about him, while the people he loved died alone. Drawing himself back into the present, he pushed the ache down deep and pushed his body ever faster, until his heart pounded and lungs burned and he had to stop, He sucked down air greedily as he walked, until his heart rate slowed and his breathing returned to normal. Taking a last look at the now sunlit buildings of Canary Wharf, he turned back towards Scott's and broke into a gentle run.

———

By 8.30 a.m. Danny was back, showered, and frying up a pack of bacon he'd found in the fridge.

'Top man. Can't beat a bacon sandwich to get the day started,' said Scott. He flicked the kettle on. 'Coffee?'

'Yeah, white, one sugar,' Danny replied.

'Yo, Scotty, same for me, mate,' came Rob's voice from the spare bedroom.

'And a bacon sandwich,' Rob added as he crossed the hall into the bathroom.

Danny smiled. It was good to be back.

Several cups of coffee later and with the bacon sandwiches all eaten, the three of them sat chatting round the dining-room table.

'So, what are your plans now?' said Scott to Danny.

'Well Paul's offered me team leader on a six-month armed escort gig. Fuel tankers going past Somalian waters. You know, threat of pirates and all that. Larger companies are still paying good money for armed escorts.'

'When does that start? You've only just got back,' said Rob, the disappointment in his voice a little too obvious.

'In about three weeks. Sorry, mate, but I need one more gig. I've nearly got enough to put down a deposit on a place, then I'll be around more, I promise,' he said winking at his brother.

'Talking of Paul,' Scott said, 'shall we have a chat with him about Amaya and CMS?'

'He's in Texas with clients this week. They're six hours or so behind, which makes it four in the morning there. We'll have to wait until later today,' said Danny, noting the disappointment in Scott's eyes.

'Steady on, Scotty boy. You've been watching too many movies. The company's probably just overstepped the mark, protecting its interests. There's a shitload of money in software, you should know that. You've made enough out of it over the years.'

'Hmm, suppose so,' said Scott.

'Tell you what,' Danny said, 'CMS is in London right. Why don't we go take a look before we bother Paul?'

Scott perked up like an excited kid about to go on an adventure.

'Ok, you two go on your road trip. Some of us have work to do,' said Rob, looking at Danny as he got up. 'I'll see you later at ours then.'

Danny chuckled. 'Yeah, I'll text you when Miss Marple here's had enough.'

CHAPTER 6

Scanning the road for impending crashes. Danny gripped the door handle as he sat snugly in the BMW's black leather Recaro sports seat. Scott had just kicked it down a gear and put his foot to the floor catapulting them rapidly into the right-hand lane of the A12. The soft-toned female voice of the satnav guiding them over the noise of the engine, towards an industrial estate on the outskirts of Stratford.

Scott's driving left Danny feeling anything but calm.

'Camera, Scotty!' he yelled.

Scott braked down to fifty just in time.

'Bloody things are ruining driving in this country.'

They'd googled CMS Software Corporation and its company director, Marcus Tenby before leaving, but hadn't found anything unusual. The website had been running for twelve years and looked like any other, corporate security software with a list of big-name clients, a company you can trust, blah blah blah. A search on Tenby hadn't turned up much either. He was listed him as company director by Companies House, there was some charity donations and an article from a university in New York written a couple of years earlier—some inspirational speech about great opportunities for IT graduates. The article included a small picture of Tenby shaking hands with a student, but it wasn't clear and his face had been partially obscured. Danny wasn't really buying the whole conspiracy theory, but it was good to be home, and great to hang out with Scott again.

After twenty minutes of buttock-clenching, seat-gripping driving, they pulled into the industrial park that was home to CMS. Most of the buildings were small- to medium-sized, and designed as modern office blocks for solicitors, IT consultants and green-energy companies. There was only the one road in ending in a turning circle for delivery lorries. Just before the circle they spotted a two-storey unit with a CMS sign above the entrance. The windows and entrance were fitted with black privacy glass preventing prying eyes from seeing inside.

Pulling up to the kerb on the opposite side of the road Scott turned off the engine. He sat staring at the building for a moment or two before speaking.

'Right, well this is awkward. I can honestly say I have no clue what we're looking for or what we're supposed to do now.'

Danny said nothing. His eyes flicked over the building, a habit acquired over the years; it was often the smallest details that were most important. There was no reception sign. The entrance doors had an intercom and a swipe-card reader. Night-and-day security cameras were mounted near the roofline on each corner, covering the building's perimeter. Nothing very surprising about that; they made security software after all. What struck him as odd was the car park. There were spaces for maybe thirty-five vehicles but only three were parked: an old Vauxhall Astra, a

Range Rover Sport with blacked-out windows, and a white Audi R8 sports car.

The spaces closer to reception had small white reservation boards. Danny could just make out titles and names. There were also empty spaces with *VISITOR* written in white paint on the tarmac. Tyre marks and oil stains marked the spots where cars had, until recently, parked up for the nine-to-five grind.

'What now?' Scott said.

The hairs on the back of Danny's neck stood up. He'd always had a sixth sense when things weren't right. It had served him well many times when on active duty and he knew better than to ignore his instincts.

'We could just go and press the buzzer, see what happens.'

'Err, yes, and say what?' Scott replied sounding a little flustered.

'You're a renowned freelance computer programmer. Ask for Marcus Tenby and make something up. Say Amaya Sato gave you his name. I don't know, tell him you think you could do some business together,' said Danny opening the door. 'Then we'll just wing it,' he added.

They reached the entrance. Even at close quarters, the black glass gave no secrets away.

Danny pressed the intercom.

'Can I help you?' The voice was tinny with a strong cockney accent.

'Scott Miller to see Marcus Tenby,' said Danny smiling up at the camera above the intercom.

'Do you have an appointment?'

'Err, yes,' he said, shrugging to Scott.

The lock buzzed open, and they pushed through the door.

The interior was small and square with a reception

desk on one side and a couple of leather sofas around a coffee table on the other. A middle-aged man with grey hair and a fat belly sat dutifully behind the desk. He stood up, revealing shiny black trousers and a cheap white shirt with a black clip on nylon tie. A Regency Security name badge etched with the words *Arthur Bunn* pinned to his breast pocket.

'If you'd like to take a seat, sirs, I'll tell him you're here,' he said, gesturing towards the sofas.

Ignoring the sofa Danny strolled over to a large viewing window on the far wall, it looked into a room almost the entire size of the ground floor. Multiple rows of data cabinets as tall as he was sat fixed in neat rows. Their little green lights blinking on and off as thousands of switches processed information, fat looms of data cables snaked in and out of the cabinets linking them all together.

'It's a server centre,' said Scott. 'All their software and client data will be routed through here.'

'How can I help you, gentlemen?' Came a voice from behind them. The man spoke softly in English with a hint of a Middle Eastern accent.

Scott and Danny turned to face a tall Arabic man, immaculately dressed in a dark tailored suit. His jet black curly hair brushed back with wet-look gel and his brown eyes glinted behind small, square, Gucci glasses. He smiled with perfect teeth through a short, precisely trimmed dense beard.

Scott stepped forward with his hand outstretched. 'Scott Miller.'

'Kadah Naser,' the man said, shaking Scott's hand. Then he turned to Danny.

'Oh. Rodger Freeman. Mr Miller's PA,' Danny said. Years of covert missions meant he'd made a few enemies along the way and he knew the value of keeping your true identity a secret.

'We're here to see Marcus Tenby,' Scott said, speaking with confidence as if he were expected.

'I'm afraid Mr Tenby is out of the country on business. Can I help you with anything?' Naser asked, his tone pleasant and business-like.

'Oh, that's a shame. I'm a colleague of Amaya Sato's. She thought we might be able to do some business together,' said Scott fishing a business card out of his pocket and passing it to Naser.

'Thank you Mr Miller, I will make sure Mr Tenby gets it,' said Naser, gesturing towards the door.

Danny stood slightly back, taking in all the details in his peripheral vision. He'd spotted a change in Naser's expression when Scott had mentioned Amaya's name. It had been small and lasted for only a split-second, but it was there all the same.

Danny and Scott left the reception area and walked slowly towards the car.

'Well, that was a waste of time,' Scott said.

'Oh, he's there. I bet he's looking out from behind that black glass as we speak,' said Danny purposely not looking back as he opened the car door.

Scott waited until they were in the car before he spoke. 'What? How do you know?'

'That place used to have twenty or thirty people working there. A server centre, you said, hence the cameras. But now nobody's there and there's a security firm being paid to babysit the building.'

Scott started the engine.

'The Astra must be the security guy's Arthur Bunn's—no way he can afford the other two cars,' Danny said, pointing to the old car. 'The Range Rover Sport has got to be Naser's. Given his height, he'd struggle to get in the R8. Which means that has to be Tenby's.' He thought for a minute. 'Let's get back to yours. I'll call Paul.'

Staring at the window on the first floor as Scott swung the car around, Danny felt the hairs on the back of his neck standing up again. He could feel the presence from behind the black glass.

CHAPTER 7

Marcus Tenby stood behind the first-floor window and watched the car pulled away through the one-way glass. It spun around in the turning circle and racing away up the road.

Kadah walked over and stood beside him, handing him Scott's business card. 'Amaya Sato again.'

Marcus didn't break his gaze. 'The data report says she made a copy of the program three weeks ago. That was the last time she logged into that PC, and I can't pull the program off her PC because she's moved it to an encrypted external folder.' He paused and frowned. 'Get Peters to find out what she's been up to. And get me that program. Then dispose of her like the others.'

The tension in the room reached breaking point and Marcus grabbed a chair, hurling it across the room, rage flashing across his face.

'Calm, my brother. We are close now. We will succeed. Trust in The Faith,' Kadah spoke calmly in Arabic as Marcus regained his composure.

'I need Sato's program. It's the last piece of the puzzle.

We cannot afford to alert suspicion before we're ready. We have to execute the plan without warning and on time,' said Marcus in Arabic. Then in perfect English he said, 'Get me Peters.'

In the corner of the room, a skinny Iranian teenager turned from his PC and looked over, a worried intense frown creasing his forehead.

'It's okay, Shan. Nothing to fret yourself about. Just carry on with your work,' Marcus said.

Shan Al Amat returned to his work. His autism made him socially awkward, but he was an exceptional programmer. At sixteen, Barzan Naser—Kadah's uncle, a preacher from a local mosque—had spotted him. He'd handpicked and groomed the more receptive members of the congregation to the ways of The Faith and the true meaning of Islam. Shan's condition had led him to fixate on Barzan's teachings, making him an easy target. Barzan had recognised Shan's talent for programming and brought him to Marcus, who'd encouraged him to work with them for the glorious good of The Faith.

CHAPTER 8

Arriving back at Scott's, Danny dialled Paul's mobile. It rang a few times then clicked and rang again. A soft voice answered—Paul's personal assistant, Trisha Fields.

'Greenwood Security.'

'Hi, Trish. It's Danny. I'm trying to get hold of Paul,' he said cheerfully. He liked Trisha and had got the feeling she'd like to get to know him a lot better too.

'Hi, Danny. Paul should be boarding a plane to London right about now. He'll be back in the office in the morning.'

'Okay. If you talk to him before then, can you tell him I'll come and see him in the morning?' It surprised him how much happier he felt after chatting to her.

'Will do, honey. See you in the morning,' she said keenly before hanging up.

Danny turned to Scott, who was steaming milk and pulling coffee shots from his expensive coffee maker.

'Paul's not back until morning. You want to come with me when I go and see him?'

'No, I can't, I'm afraid. I've got some important conference calls to Milan,' he said, sprinkling cocoa powder through a plastic stencil to form the perfect coffee-bean shape on top of the froth.

'You know as much as I do, old boy. I'll make you a copy of the program Amaya sent to give to Paul.'

Scott brought the coffee over to Danny at the dining table.

'Okay, mate. But don't get all conspiracy-theorist on me. Chances are there's no mystery, no cloak and dagger. Just a logical explanation.'

He'd been thinking it over. Apart from things being a little odd at CMS, there was nothing to suggest that anything sinister was taking place.

Sipping his drink Danny looked at his watch. 'I must get going soon. I've got to get the Tube and then a bus back to Rob's.'

'Here you go. Take the car. And try to bring it back in one piece,' said Scott tossing the keys to his BMW across the table.

'You never know, you might impress the luscious Trisha turning up in that,' he chuckled.

'Cheers, Scotty. Are you sure, mate?'

'Quite sure. I've still got the Porsche if I need to go anywhere, now I must get on with some work.' Said Scott disappearing to his office while Danny headed for the guest room.

He packed his wash bag and clothes back into his army backpack, then went to find Scott. He was busy in his office, typing furiously while browsing an array of open windows on three large monitors mounted around him in a semi circle. It all looked like gibberish to Danny—lines of commands, instructions and symbols.

'Program code. Amaya's. I'm putting it onto a new memory stick.'

'If you say so.'

'Here you are, you caveman. The entry fob and door keys are on there. Let yourself in when you come back,' said Scott passing the keys and the flash drive over his shoulder before returning to his keyboard.

'Cheers, Scotty. See you tomorrow, mate.'

———

Pushing the fire door open, Danny took the stairs rather than the lift to the underground car park. Old habits again. He had an aversion to being stuck in confined spaces with only one exit. A little voice in his head from his years in the SAS screamed potential kill box. He pressed the release button at the bottom of the stairwell and pushed the heavy fire door to the underground parking open. Smiling, he climbed into the M4. The powerful engine started with a satisfying growl, he drove up the ramp pulling out into the London traffic enjoying his friend's choice of car. Late afternoon crept into early evening. After driving carefully across the capital, he rolled up outside the house he'd grown up in. He'd let Rob have the house after their mother died. It had been a bad time, his mother was in hospital with terminal cancer and his wife and child had recently died. He'd gone into a self- destructive spiral, chasing dangerous missions and throwing himself into combat situations that should have killed him. Somehow he'd survived long enough to get his head together. He left the regiment shortly afterwards, coming home in time to see his mum before she died. Danny grabbed his backpack from the boot and walked up the drive smiling as he passed

Tina's car. He liked Rob's girlfriend and loved seeing his little brother happy and in love.

When he entered the hall of the old Georgian four-bedroom semi, the atmosphere and smell transported him back to his childhood. The decor might have changed, but the memories of him and Rob flying up and down the stairs or playing football in the back garden always came flooding back. Happy times.

Hearing voices in the kitchen, he wandered on through.

'Evening all,' he said cheerily.

'Danny, it's good to see you,' said Tina giving him a big hug and kiss on the cheek.

'Wanna beer, bro?' said Rob, opening the fridge.

'Yeah, thanks, Rob.'

Danny drew out a chair at the kitchen table. 'How's life with you, Tina? Still planning on marrying this idiot?'

'Life is great with me thank you very much, and he may be an idiot, but he's *my* idiot,' Tina said with a smile that lit up the room.

'I am here, you know,' said Rob, feigning hurt.

Tina turned to Danny. 'August 23rd for the wedding. Make sure you're around.'

'Hmm, I'll probably be on a boat somewhere in the Gulf but I'll book a week off.'

'You better,' Rob said. 'You're the best man.'

'What, really? Not Scott or your mate Barney? I'd be honoured,' said Danny, bursting with pride.

They ate and chatted into the night until tiredness sent them all to bed. With a few beers in him and high on his brother's happiness, Danny had one of the best sleeps in ages.

CHAPTER 9

At 2.15 a.m. in central Berlin, Erich Schneider stumbled out of Bricks nightclub on Mohrenstrasse. He'd been out celebrating with friends. The completion of a two-year contract meant he was expecting a large payout. Waving off his friends, he wobbled slowly toward his apartment. He'd walked about half a kilometre when a taxi passed by, pulling up a short distance ahead of him. Erich ambled on without taking much notice, a stocky South American man—or maybe he was Mexican—in jeans and a bomber jacket got out the back and bent down to the front window, presumably to pay the driver. When Erich got within a few metres, the man stood, turned and walked briskly past him. Even in Erich's drunken state, the man's stature and body language unsettled him; he'd turned his head a fraction, exposing a deep vertical scar that ran from the centre of his eyebrow to the middle of his cheek. His eyes, dark and lifeless, met Erich's as they passed, sending a chill down his spine. Thankful that he'd passed the man without incident, Erich drew level with the taxi's open window.

A low gravelly voice came from within. 'Hey, mate, you wanna taxi?'

The English threw him. Although he spoke it fluently, he hadn't been expecting to hear it from a local taxi.

He stooped down to look through the window. 'Excuse me?'

The driver seemed to fill the front of the cab. A head turned on the largest neck Erich had ever seen and smiled. Erich opened his mouth to speak again but was silenced by a massive punch to the kidneys. The pain knocked the air out of him. Another punch landed low on the other side. He doubled up as every ounce of wind was forced from his lungs. The pain was crippling. The back door of the taxi opened and the man with the scar threw him hard across the seat climbing in behind him.

'Evening, Fritz. Where do you wanna go?' Snipe said with a chuckle.

'Come on. Stop fucking about,' Ramirez said as he landed a powerful punch to Erich's temple.

'I think you've got anger issues, Rami, me old mate,' said Snipe still chuckling as he pulled away.

———

A mile away Peters and Smith loaded a box and two big tool bags into a white Transit van outside Erich's apartment. The decal on the side read

24-Hour Call-Out, P. Smit, Plumbing and Heating Engineers

They'd stolen it a couple of hours ago. Erich's CMS computer was in the box, while his phones, memory sticks, hard drives and CMS paperwork had been packed into the tool bags. Smith climbed in the driver's seat and Peters took the passenger side. He held up his buzzing mobile and answered it as Smith pulled away into the early morning quiet.

'Yes.'

'There's been a change of plan.' said Marcus in his customary soft, perfect English. 'We have to move the Tokyo contract forward. She's no longer performing and may have involved other parties.'

Peters was sure he'd detected a hint of annoyance in Marcus's voice which was unusual.

'Finish up there and get to Brandenburg Airport. There's a private jet on standby. It'll take you to Tokyo. I'll give you further instructions shortly.'

———

Across the city in the commercial district, Snipe turned down a dark, quiet road that ran in front of some industrial units. Snipe and Ramirez had checked the place out earlier for cameras or late workers, the River Spree could be seen twinkling in the moonlight behind the units at the end of the road. He pulled up on the kerb as close to the river as he could get and killed the lights. Ramirez opened the door and dragged Erich onto the tarmac. The man wept while as he wheezed and coughed, a dark stain appeared as he pissed his pants. Ramirez knelt on his chest and rifled through his pockets. He found a wallet and a phone and passed them to Snipe.

'Fucking stop snivelling. Shut the fuck up,' Snipe said kicking Erich hard in the face.

His nose exploded as the cartilage gave way. Blood poured down his face. Snipe grabbed the semi-conscious body and dragged it along as though he were taking out the trash. He headed for the river's edge, towards the dark space between two industrial units.

'Wait. Let me get his ring and watch first,' Ramirez said, grabbing Erich's arm firmly.

At the back of the units was a concrete docking area with a two-metre drop to the cold, dark, fast-flowing water.

'Make it look like a mugging gone wrong. Not too clean,' said Ramirez.

Snipe grinned and eased a six-inch serrated blade from a sheath attached to his belt. Erich opened his eyes. They went wide in terror as the moonlight glinted off the blade, Snipe thumped the blade into his chest, then out. As the thrill of the kill took him he repeated the action with lightning speed, moving to the abdomen, like a boxer letting loose a torrent of punches. Erich tried to pull the breath in to scream. His mouth went through the motions, but nothing came out. The last thing he saw before the darkness closed in on him was Snipe's insane face.

'Bye, Fritz,' Snipe said, throwing him into the river.

Ramirez got into the driver's seat of the taxi and scanned the road for witnesses. The road was still dark and still quiet. Snipe climbed in the back and wiped the blood off his knife as the cab pulled off into the night. He text Peters: *All done*. The phone rang back within seconds.

'You're behind schedule. The warehouse. Ten minutes,' said Peters in his usual monotone. 'There's been a change of plan.'

Snipe listened as Peters relayed the new details, then hung up. Gritting his teeth, he looked down at his glinting knife, murder in his eyes.

'Warehouse, Rami. Apparently, we're fucking late. Ten minutes, mate. Step on it. We're off to Tokyo.' He sheathed the knife and muttered, 'One day I'll shut that wanker up for good.'

CHAPTER 10

anny rolled over in bed for his G-Shock watch—
5.50 a.m. Better. He tried to get another hours
sleep but gave after ten minutes and he got up.
Pulling on his shorts and t-shirt he went for a run.

The weather was cool but not cold and the early morning sky was mostly pale blue with just a few cotton wool clouds for company. As the world woke up he pounded the streets of Walthamstow. First down Boundary Road, past the rows of homogeneous terraced houses, their windows, porches and doors painted in a multitude of different colours—people's little piece of Britain with their small stamp of individuality. He moved along under the railway bridge and turned right down Hoe Street towards the centre of town. Passed the ground-floor shops and businesses, topped with flats. He ran past the gym, run by his friend and local legend, Big Dave Pullman, carrying on passed the schools and parks that triggered childhood memories. Without concious thought he found himself outside his old marital home. They had changed the windows and the front door was a different colour, but he could still visualise Sarah and Timmy waving him off from the front door.

Back on Walthamstow High Street, he reached the crossroads where his wife had been driving his son home from school. A lorry had hit them side-on at speed. It flipped and crushed the small car, then driven off without stopping. Timmy was killed on impact. Sarah had lived for a further half an hour passing away as the firemen raced to cut her out. Danny played out the accident in his mind as though it were happening in front of him. Fresh pain flooded back like an open wound, halting him until he could push it down deep inside.

He tore himself away, running hard along the high street, back towards the sanctuary of his mother old house.

Breathing hard and dripping with sweat, he shut the front door softly, not sure if Rob or Tina were awake. The sound of laughter from the kitchen answering his question. It was a welcome distraction, and he walked through to join the happy couple.

'Morning, bro. I wondered where you were. You want coffee?'

'Please. Pour us one while I grab a shower. I'll be down in a minute,' Danny replied.

Fifteen minutes later he was sitting at the table, showered and shaved, water still dripping down the back of his neck from his damp hair. They had breakfast together. The cheery atmosphere lifted his mood and kicked him back into reality. Tina kissed Rob goodbye and left for work. She was based in the high-street branch of Barclays Bank. Danny offered to clear the breakfast things away leaving Rob to disappear upstairs to the back bedroom that he'd set up as an office.

Dishes done, Danny checked the time and went upstairs. He popped his head round Rob's door.

'Work's going well then?' he said, pleased to see Rob surrounded by papers and files labelled with different company names.

'Yeah, thanks to Scott. He's given me personal introductions to some of his biggest customers.' Rob spun his chair around. 'You know, you don't have to go away again. I can help you out with a place. This house should be half yours, anyway.'

'Thanks, Rob, but this is yours. You were there for mum all those years while I was away. You deserve it. End of.' He wasn't going to discuss it any further. 'Anyway, it's one last gig. I'll be sitting on my arse soaking up the sun. The Somali pirates don't bother ships with an armed escort. Wave a gun and they bugger off,' said Danny smiling at his brother. 'Look, it's shitloads of money for doing nothing. I'll come back the week before the wedding and I'll be finished and back for good by Christmas.' He slapped Rob on the shoulder.

'Okay, okay,' Rob said, but Danny could hear the reluctance in his voice.

'Right, I'm off to see Paul about Scott's friend, and then I'm taking Scott's car back. I'll be back teatime.'

The sports car started with a throaty rumble. He dropped it into gear and headed for Islington.

———

They'd met in Afghanistan. Danny was a sergeant in the SAS, leading covert missions against key targets in the hunt for Osama Bin Laden. Paul Greenwood was an officer in the intelligence corps. His reputation for accuracy and correctly calling situations had made him the main man everyone wanted in their camp.

The two had become good friends and had worked

together for several years and on many missions. It was during that time a convoy was attacked on the way back to camp. Paul and his driver were taken captive by Al Qaeda fighters. Disobeying a direct order to stay put, Danny and his unit went to rescue them. The five soldiers raided the armoury and snuck out of camp in a stolen Nissan pickup truck. After four days in the hills, they drove out of the badlands and back to base camp…A tortured Paul and his driver lying in the flatbed, weak but alive.

As commanding officer, Danny took the rap for the unauthorised mission. To his surprise, he'd escaped a court martial with a call from Whitehall to the base commander making the whole thing go away. Paul, it seemed, was rather well connected even back then.

When Danny left the regiment, Paul offered him work in his new security business and he'd been there ever since. Although Danny had never asked for or expected anything from Paul, he'd been grateful for his help and friendship over the years.

CHAPTER 11

Rush hour. Danny barely managed to get out of second gear, and the journey to Paul's office took the best part of an hour. Greenwood Security was located on the third floor of an old Victorian building, shared with a firm of accountants on the ground floor and an insurance company on the first and second. Ignoring the tiny old lift, a nineteen fifties add on built into the middle of the square staircase, he bounded up the steps two at a time before entered the squeaky oak doors of Greenwood Security. Expecting to see Emma on reception, he was taken back by a new face.

'Good morning, sir. How can I help you?' she said cheerfully.

He was just about to ask for Paul when Trisha's dulcet tones floated across the room.

'Don't worry, Lucy. This is Danny Pearson,' she said, tottering as fast as she could in her high heels and tight skirt.

'Nice to meet you. You're a legend around here,' Lucy

said. Her wide smile displayed two rows of perfect white teeth.

Trisha passed the reception desk and gave Danny her customary big hug. He returned the embrace, breathing in the sweet perfume she was wearing. He had to admit, she looked, smelled and felt great.

'Nice to meet you, Lucy. And lovely to see you as always, Trish,' he said feeling his face flush.

'Paul's just on the phone. He'll be done in a minute. Come on through and I'll make you a drink,' she said noticing his embarrassment.

Danny followed, trying not to stare at her wiggling bum as she walked. Paul spotted him while talking on the phone and stood beckoning him in to sit.

After taking drinks orders, Trisha spun on her heels and left. She returned with the coffees just as Paul hung up.

'Thanks, Trish... Danny nice to see you.' Paul stood and reached over the desk to shake his hand. 'You're going to take the boat job, yes?'

'Yes, but that's not why I'm here. I'm after a favour,' Danny said, picking up his drink as Trisha left.

'I'm all ears. What can I help you with?' said Paul sitting back in his chair, intrigued.

Danny went through the events of the past few days, starting with Amaya contacting Scott for help with the program she'd been working on, and concluding with their unscheduled visit to CMS.

Paul listened, tumbling the memory stick Danny had given him between his fingers. When he'd finished, Paul stared at the little silver stick in his hands saying nothing for a few minutes. Danny waited patiently. He knew how Paul worked, the way he digested every detail and knitted it into a bigger picture.

Eventually Paul put down the flash drive and looked up. 'I'll make a few calls,' he said without further comment.

'I don't want to waste your time, Paul. I promised Scott I'd ask. CMS just didn't feel right. There was something about that guy Kadah Naser I didn't like.'

'No, it's fine. I'll look in to it.'

Pocketing the memory stick, Paul smiled and changed the subject. They talked for a while about the armed-escort job for the boats. Danny told him about Rob's wedding and how he wanted to buy a house and stay put for a while after the boat gig. Paul was glad his friend had reached a point where he wanted to put down roots again, he'd secretly been waiting until Danny was in the right head space to offer him a permanent place in the company. A man of Danny's talents was incredibly useful in the planning of his high-profile security customers' needs—and not to mention the needs of his more discreet customers. They were still talking an hour later when Trisha brought more coffee in. As she handed a cup to Danny, her hand lingered just a second too long, causing him to look up, slightly flustered.

'Err, thanks, Trish.'

'You're welcome,' she said, tottering out of the office.

'When are you going to ask that girl out?' Paul asked, once Trisha was out of earshot.

'I was just wondering the same thing myself,' said Danny looking at his watch. 'I've got to go. Give us a ring if any of that Amaya stuff comes to anything,' he said rising from his seat as he gulped the last of his drink down.

'Will do,' said Paul standing to shake his hand.

Danny left Paul's office, but instead of heading for the exit he walked over to Trisha's desk.

'I don't suppose you'd like to go out to dinner one night

this week?' he said. His palms feeling sweaty and his heart beating fast like an anxious school kid's.

'I would love to. How about tomorrow night?' She smiled and took her phone out of her bag.

Danny was all fingers and thumbs as he punched in her number. He kissed her on the cheek then turned and walked out of the office with a big grin on his face.

———

Paul watched from his office and smiled. Then he picked up his phone and hit one of the speed-dial buttons. They answered his call within two rings.

'Jenkins.'

'Edward, it's Paul. I need the tech guys to look at something. We have Tokyo to add to the list, and this time I have a program.'

CHAPTER 12

igh above the East China Sea, a Gulfstream G550 was on its final approach to Narita Airport, Tokyo. The men on board relaxed in the spacious cabin of the executive jet. Smith sat at one table, looking at home in a tailored grey pinstripe suit from Savile Row. He tinkered with a surveillance bug the size of a bottle top, tweaking and measuring the volume levels on his laptop. Ramirez and Snipe lounged in the reclining leather seats, drinking beer. Both wore black suits and white shirts with black ties. Their jackets hung over the backs of their seats, CMS Software Corporation security badges clipped to the lapels. Peters' suit was cut from dark blue cloth, as expensive as Smith's and from the same Savile Row tailor.

He studied the files and photos of Amaya Sato and her boyfriend Eito Hamisaki. His fixer, Hamish, had supplied him with a wealth of information on this target, as he had for all the contracts. He'd also provided full IDs for each member of the team—passports, driving licences, credit cards—and burner phones. Peters needed to wrap this up quickly. Marcus had been uncharacteristically rattled by Amaya's excuses for not completing her contract. And now her PC was offline, effectively cutting off their eyes and ears. Perhaps she was double-crossing him and planning to sell the program to the highest bidder. Peters didn't know, but he'd find out by whatever means necessary. He had no idea what Marcus's grand plan was, but no one went to this much expense and effort to cover their tracks without having something big planned. It wasn't his problem, and he really didn't care. It was just another job with a very large pay cheque. He could deal with the pressure from Marcus; what he didn't like was the lack of planning time.

Because of its complications and the tight timescale, he'd demanded twice the usual fee. Amaya Sato was the last of seven names on Peters' list and marked the end of his business arrangement with Marcus Tenby. He planned to disappear to some faraway country once this was over. He had enough money to quit this life, buy the place of his dreams and live a quiet, comfortable life. As for the others, he wasn't sure. Smith was an intelligent man—he'd have an exit plan for sure. Ramirez had talked of buying a small coffee plantation in South America. As for Snipe, Peters was in no doubt that things would end badly. He'd become increasingly difficult to handle and his psychotic behaviour was more than worrying. He'd keep on killing; he enjoyed it too much. And when this was over, Peters wanted to get as far away from Snipe as possible.

He turned his attention back to the folder and the mission at hand.

As soon as they landed, the surveillance on Sato would begin and the details of his plan would be checked and double-checked. Piss-poor planning led to piss-poor performance, and mistakes caused mission failures. Peters accepted neither.

CHAPTER 13

I n the unused upstairs offices at CMS, Marcus and Shan finished praying. They stood, rolled up their prayer mats and placed them in the cupboard. Then they slid their shoes on.

'You are a good boy, Shan,' Marcus said. 'Allah will reward you for your devotion.'

Shan gave a faint smile for a brief second before resuming his usual look of intense concentration.

'Soon, there will be a very special mission for you Shan. The Faith has chosen you, and you alone. We have plans to make, my friend.' Marcus put his hand on Shan's shoulder, speaking as a father would to his child. 'You must talk to no one but me about this. Not Barzan or Kadah. No one. Do you understand?' Marcus stared hard at Shan, searching for confirmation. To his surprise, Shan spoke.

'I understand, Marcus. Only you.'

'Good. We'll talk about this later. Now it's back to work on those link programs.'

They returned to the rows of computer monitors streaming with programming code.

CHAPTER 14

I t was coming up to midday by the time Danny pulled into the underground car park at Scott's. The exhaust echoed loudly off the concrete as he rolled up next to the Porsche. The electronic fob got him through the heavy yellow fire door, he took the stairs to Scott's apartment two at a time, enjoying the explosive release of energy as his legs powered upwards. With his pulse raised but not racing, he reached the apartment door and unlocked it.

'You here, Scotty?'

'Back here, in the office old man,' came Scott's muffled reply.

Danny made his way to Scott's office and found him screen-hopping from emails to search engine results to photos. His desk and the work table were covered in print-outs of articles, pictures and news reports.

'What's all this?' Danny said, glancing at some papers.

'Aha! I couldn't sleep last night, so I started digging up information on CMS. Found some pretty interesting stuff.' He handed Danny several sheets. 'That picture there is a company photo for a trade magazine from just over three years ago. It shows around forty employees outside the CMS building.'

He tapped the picture in Danny's hand and pointed to one of the people in it.

'That gentleman with the grey suit is Chris Mayhew. He was the director at the time they took the picture.' He pointed to a copy of a newspaper report. 'Sometime shortly after that, Mayhew's wife and children died in a house fire while he was away on business.' Scott was on a roll now, tapping the two other sheets of text in Danny's other hand. 'Those are social media posts from employees. They say how tragic the fire was and how nobody has seen Mayhew since. Look at these Facebook posts— they're from staff talking about their surprise as Mayhew announced his retirement from CMS, with the managing directors position being appointed to program develop-ment manager Marcus Tenby. Stranger still, the news was announced by a letter read out by Tenby himself. Nobody has seen Mayhew since.'

Scott swivelled his seat around and enlarged several windows containing the trade articles and Facebook conversations.

'Okay, leap forward to three months ago. Tenby has shed half the workforce over a two-year period. Then he announces that the company is merging with some Amer-ican software giant, resulting in the closure of the London office. That makes the last remaining employees redundant.'

Danny spent a few seconds looking at the monitors and taking in all the information.

'Shit, Scott. How did you find all this?'

Scott looked up, grinning. 'I told you, old man, I'm the dog's bollocks. What I find curious is that shortly after Tenby becomes managing director, he outsources work to

Amaya when throughout the previous year he's been systematically laying off staff whose job it was to do that sort of programming in-house.'

'Yeah, that's definitely strange. Did you find anything else on Mayhew after he handed over?' Danny said, his senses tingling. There was something very wrong going on at CMS.

'No, nothing. No social media, no articles, no registration of anything new with Companies House, and none of my contacts have heard of him working with any other software companies.'

'Can you send this to Paul? He'll know what to do with it,' said Danny putting down the papers and looked at his watch. 'Do you fancy a pub lunch, mate?'

'I thought you'd never ask.'

Scott gathered his findings together and emailed them to Paul.

'Oh, and while we're there, you can tell me a good place to take someone on a date,' said Danny, waiting for the third degree. Scott just smiled like a Cheshire cat.

UNTITLED

16

Raiden Hamisaki left through the back door of a sleazy massage parlour in the heart of Kabukicho, Tokyo's red-light district. He swaggered down the thin alley towards a waiting blue Subaru Impreza.

Feeling good in his new Adidas trainers, jeans and Superdry t-shirt. Raider hid his eyes behind wrap-around Ray-Bans even though it was night. A sharp Superdry leather jacket finished the outfit off. He'd purposely left it half undone to allow a glimpse of the Glock 17 hand gun swinging in a holster under his left arm... partly in case anyone was having second thoughts about paying, or one of the girls' clients got too nosey, but mostly because it made him feel feared and respected. It was a feeling he'd grown to like and crave, though in truth it wasn't him the massage parlour and brothel owners feared. He was just a low-level bag man for the Yakuza organised crime syndi-cate. The people he worked for were known for showing no mercy. They dished out harsh punishments and frequently killed those who crossed them.

News stories of drive-by shootings and executions were commonplace across the city. The Uzi sub-machine gun being their weapon of choice. You didn't cross the Yakuza.

Climbing into the Subaru Raiden slumped down low in the seat. He casually pointed forward, indicating for the driver to pull away. The cars throaty exhaust gurgled as the headed for a meet a couple of streets away. Pulling alongside another car, he handed the bag of cash to the passenger of another car, who in turn would do the same, moving it up the chain.

That's the way it went night after night, money and drugs never staying in one place too long. Man to man, car to car, making it hard for the authorities to follow, and impossible for them to reach the men at the top. A couple of miles further on Raiden's driver pulled up alongside a custom Nissan Skyline. The window came down to revealing a spotty-faced teenager with shades and a baseball cap. He nodded at Raiden who returned the gesture as he took a package off him containing small bags of cocaine. The windows went up, and both cars pulled away in different directions.

His mobile rang and brief instructions were conveyed. He hung up and gave the address to his driver. The Subaru gurgled down the street before swinging right towards its next destination.

Fifty metres back, a tall figure in black leathers watched through the mirrored visor of his helmet. He accelerated his motorbike a little before turning right to follow the Subaru at a discreet distance.

———

Raiden's mobile rang again, he tried to lift his Ray-Bans to look at the caller ID without the driver seeing, he didn't want to ruin his cool image. Once he saw it was his cousin calling he dropped the shades back down and answered.

'Eito, how you doin'?' He said listening as Eito talked. 'She's got to chill out, cuz. That geeky computer shit's gone to her head. Proper paranoid, man.'

The car pulled up beside a long dark alley leading to Raiden's next drop-off point. His driver waited patiently as Raiden talked.

'No worries. Yeah, I'll bring some weed round later. Tell Amaya to chill, man.'

He hung up and got out of the car. Adjusting his shades, he swaggered into the alley, passing several doors before being engulfed in darkness. He approached the dimly lit rear entrance of his next drop and the destination of his package—cocaine to keep the brothel's punters merry and encourage them to part with more of their hard-earned cash.

'Good evening.'

Raiden spun around to face the suppressed barrel of a fully automatic Uzi sub- machine gun. He froze, all the swagger and bravado gone. Fear of what might be coming gripped him.

'Go for your gun,' the stranger said calmly, his visor only half-open, allowing him to be heard without offering any clues to the man inside.

'No, no, no, take it,' Raiden said, offering the package of drugs.

'Take your gun out now.'

Leaning in the stranger pushed the barrel of the gun closer to Raiden's head. 'Whoa, okay, okay.' Feeling a small tear run down his cheek from under his Ray-Bans. Raiden reached slowly into his jacket with a shaky hand and pulled the Glock out, gripping the handle between his fingers. His hand trembled as he held it by his side keeping it pointed firmly at the ground. Shame overcame fear as he lost control of his bladder and felt a warm wet patch spreading down his trouser leg.

'Oh, that's embarrassing,' the stranger said, letting off a burst of hissing fire. It knocked Raiden back off his feet as a dozen rounds ripped through his head and chest.

He was dead before he hit the ground.

His limp body oozing with blood. One of the bullets had gone straight through the lens of his Ray-Bans a tear of blood replacing its watery twin.

The rider picked up the package and stuffed it into his jacket, before riffling through Raiden's pockets. He located the phone and sent a text, then threw the device onto the floor by the body.

Satisfied he turned and ran through the shadows of the dark alley towards the Subaru, the Uzi pointed straight ahead.

Sitting bored in the car Raiden's driver glanced down the alley into the darkness. Had he heard something over the gurgling of the Subaru's exhaust? Just as he decided it was nothing the biker erupted out of the shadows, unleashing a hail of automatic fire instantly ripping the car and driver to shreds.

Bystanders on the street screamed and ran for cover, diving into shops and restaurants or crouching behind parked vehicles.

The rider tossed the Uzi calmly to the ground and got back on his bike, before screaming off into the night.

CHAPTER 15

Eito lay on Amaya's bed watching TV smiling to himself. He'd spent the last hour in bed making up with Amaya, and was lying there satisfied while she took a shower. He looked at the bedside alarm clock for the third time in ten minutes. When was Raiden going to drop off that weed? It had been a tense week, and he needed a smoke to mellow the weekend out. Amaya had been on edge all week, convinced she was being spied on. She'd even unplugged her PC from the mains and wouldn't let him turn it back on. Eito couldn't understand why she didn't just finish the stupid program and take the money. A sound from the living room caught his ear. Faint and rhythmic. Tap tap tap. He slid off the bed and pulled on his underwear. Tap tap tap. Following the sound, he padded through to the lounge.

Snipe was sitting on the sofa, his feet up on the coffee table, tapping the nozzle of the suppressed Uzi lightly against the wall beside him. Behind him, Ramirez was busy rifling through Amaya's computer desk. Eito stopped short, rooted to the spot in fear and surprise, no clue what to do. He wasn't given the time to think about it; Snipe squeezed off a blast of automatic fire throwing Eito into the wall behind him. The suppressor dampened the sound to nothing more than a rapid succession of metallic pings.

'Eito!' came a faint call from the en-suite bathroom. 'Eito, what was that noise?'

Snipe rose slowly from the sofa, huge and menacing like a creature of nightmares.

'Coming, dear,' he whispered.

'Snipe.' Ramirez looked up from Eito's phone giving him a warning look.

'Yeah, yeah. I'll find out what she's been up to first,' Snipe said, walking slowly towards the bedroom.

Ramirez shook his head and returned to the messages.

———

A few miles away a mobile buzzed from a puddle of blood. A full message history between Eito and Raiden appeared... a history of meetings and deals and double-crossings. All pointing to a Yakuza revenge hit.

———

Outside Amaya's apartment block, the motorbike pulled to a stop. Smith emerged from the shadows to meet it. Flipping the visor up Peters unzipped his jacked and handed the package to him.

'All's good. Has Hamish hacked the phones yet?' Peters said, looking at his watch.

Smith tucked the package away and cleaned his little round glasses on his shirt. 'Yes, boss. He's just texted to say it's done.'

'Good, find out what she's been up to. Then get the program clean the place and get out,' Peters said.

'Okay, boss.' Smith said turning towards the door.

Peters caught his arm as he went. 'Keep an eye on Snipe. I don't want any fuck-ups. Ok.'

Smith nodded and turned away as Peters rode off to ditch the bike.

CHAPTER 16

Marcus sat in a large black leather chair behind a walnut-veneered desk. From the director's office he could see the empty desks and chairs that had once been filled by programmers and technicians —ordinary men and women who'd expected long years of employment. That was before he'd orchestrated a takeover and a slew of redundancies. His gaze darted up to the clock on the wall. It'd only been five minutes since he'd last looked. The minutes were passing painfully slowly and his nerves were fraying. He needed news from Peters, needed Amaya's program, needed to know who she'd been talking to, needed to complete the master program. But most of all, he needed to regain control of the situation and get his plans back on track. Kadah came up the stairs and weaved through the empty office space towards him.

'I got you some food, brother. You need to keep your strength up.' Kadah smiled as he handed Marcus a bag from Subway.

'Thank you, but I cannot eat.' Marcus's voice cracked slightly.

'Calm yourself. Trust in Allah. He is protecting us on our journey. Now eat.' Kadah slid the sandwich closer to Marcus, who reluctantly took a bite.

The ringing of the phone cut through the silence, making them both jump. Marcus grabbed it. 'Yes?'

'Yoseph, it's Barzan. I've had contact from Akbar. The motherland wants to know if you will be ready in time.' Barzan spoke nervously, his voice betraying his fear of Akbar Bakr and The Faith leaders.

'Not now, Uncle. And don't call me Yoseph. I gave up that identity years ago, as I will give up this one once this is over.' Marcus tried to remain calm. He didn't need Barzan's complaining right now; he needed to talk to Peters.

Barzan began to whine but Marcus cut him short.

'Not now. I will call you later,' he said angrily and hung up.

Barzan had taken Marcus in when his parents were killed in an American bombing raid during the Gulf War. He'd been at university by then.

Born Yoseph Mosul, his parents had sent him to boarding school in England. There he'd met Kadah, his roommate, and best and only friend. Kadah's Uncle Barzan was the preacher at a local mosque and had raised them in the faith. In return, the boys had used their education and skills to develop subversive ways of communicating through the dark net with their Al Qaeda brothers who later split and became The Faith, led by Akbar Bakr. His thoughts of the past vanished when his mobile rang again. The screen displayed the long-awaited number.

'Yes,' Marcus said impatiently.

'We have a problem,' said Peters.

'Go on.'

'The girl has finished the program. It was encrypted

and stored on her boyfriend's laptop. She gave us a false password that put the laptop into a data dump. There's nothing left. The data's been deleted.'

'How could you let this happen? You bunch of amateur imbeciles!'

'Wait. There's a copy. We found out she'd been in contact with an old colleague in London and sent it to him.'

'Who? Who has my program?' yelled Marcus.

'His name is Scott Miller. He's some high-profile programmer.'

After several moments of uneasy silence Marcus spoke. His voice was calm and composed.

'I'll have the plane ready. Miller was here a few days ago, sniffing around with his assistant. Get back here. Get the program and get rid of Miller.'

Marcus hung up. He took Miller's business card and spun it in his fingers.

Kadah looked at him, waiting for him to take command of the situation. Although it had never been discussed or decided, Marcus's superior intellect and dominant character had enabled him to grow from a student to the leader. It was Marcus who'd planned the events they were so close to executing. It was an idea he'd been dreaming of since his parents had been killed.

Marcus met Kadah's gaze. 'Who was the man that came here with Miller?'

'His PA. He said his name was Rodger Freeman. He did not look like a PA to me. There was something about the way he moved,' said Kadah thoughtfully. 'Strong, dangerous, like Peters' men. Trained and alert.'

'I agree. We need to move our plans forward and use Mr Smith's talents as discussed,' said Marcus. 'Get Miller's details to Peters along with a picture of his face from the CCTV recordings.'

'How soon after we get Amaya's program can the master be ready for the test?' Kadah said.

'Three, maybe four days, with Shan, you, me and Barzan's three recruits working on it. We must prep the server site,' said Marcus, fighting to keep his nerves in check. The new players presented an increased risk. Still, Amaya's program was only a small piece of the puzzle, and on its own would not be enough to alert anyone to his scheme.

CHAPTER 17

Danny pulled up outside the neat, white-painted Georgian townhouse. It sat in a street of identical homes in Highbury, North London. Scott had insisted Danny take his car for the date with Trisha. After their pub lunch he'd dragged Danny round the shops, making him buy a new outfit, before pushing him into a barber shop for a haircut and shave. Although Danny had complained vigorously, he had to admit he looked considerably better for the enforced makeover. He got out of the car and brushed his hands over his charcoal Armani jeans and checked that his blue Ralph Lauren shirt was tucked in. Then he walked up to the door and pressed the bell. He waited nervously, like a school kid picking up his prom date. Through the frosted glass panel, he saw Trisha's silhouette approach. She opened the door.

'Hi,' she said with a smile that could have lit up the darkest room.

'Hi,' he said, and paused. 'Shall we go?' He gestured for her to go ahead of him. She wore a knee-length black dress that showed off her curves, and a cream cardigan to keep out the evening chill. Her black heels clicked on the path as she walked, and Danny couldn't help but stare at the seam of her stockings—a perfectly straight line that drew Danny's eye to her shapely legs. He side-stepped around her to open the car door.

'Mm, nice,' she said.

'I can't lie—it's Scott's. You remember Scott?' He shut the door and circled around to the driver's side.

'Isn't he the one whose wife found him in bed with a young Chinese student?' Trisha said.

'Japanese actually, but yes, that's him.' He smiled back and started the engine. 'Hopefully, he's got better taste in restaurants than he has in women. He's got us a reservation at The Fenchurch.'

'Really? The one in the building with the Sky Garden?' said Trisha.

'Err, yes. It's on the thirty-seventh floor. Is that okay?' Danny said.

'Yes, it's very okay. I've always wanted to go there,' she said, beaming.

Scott's choice turned out to be first class. The panoramic views of London's night-time skyline were stunning, and although Danny was more of a steak and chips and a pint man, the à la carte menu was amazing.

He listened intently as Trisha talked, mesmerised by her deep-blue eyes and wavy blonde hair. She talked about her life and her divorce. Danny didn't talk too much about his past—Trisha already knew all about the death of his wife and son. Instead, he spoke with glowing pride about Rob and his approaching wedding to Tina, and his plans to buy a place when he finished his next job. After three exquisite courses and coffee, he drove her home. Feeling like a teenager, the first-date nerves built. Had the date gone well? What would be the best way to say goodnight?

They pulled up outside Trisha's house and he leapt out of the car and around to open the door for her. As she climbed out, he offered his hand.

'Thank you. Quite the gentleman,' she said. Her hand lingered in his for a few seconds as he walked her to the door.

She put the key in the lock and clicked it open.

'I've had a wonderful night. Would you like to come in for a nightcap?' She placed her hand lightly on his arm.

'Yes, if that's okay,' he said.

Trisha slid her hand down his arm and took his hand in hers. With a smile she led him into the hall and closed the door. She kicked off her heels and turned, stood up on tiptoes, then slid her hands up behind his neck and pulled him towards her. Her kiss was soft and tender, the sweet smell of her perfume and heat from her gentle hands on his neck intoxicating. Passion he hadn't experienced for a long time stirred within him as he embraced her. Trisha pulled gently away, slid her hand down to take his, and took a step up the stairs.

'Are you sure?' he said, just above a whisper.

She smiled and took another step, then one more. He followed her nervously into the bedroom. As they kissed passionately, she undid the buttons on his shirt then eased it off his shoulders. She faltered for a second, his scars throwing her.

'Sorry. Do they bother you?' he said.

'No, I knew you'd seen action and been wounded. I just didn't realise how much.' She moved one hand over the three bullet-wound scars on his left side and caressed the various shrapnel and knife marks on his right side with the other. Then she kissed his chest and his neck and turned.

'Unzip me.'

He slowly pulled the zip to the base of her spine, noticing her smooth skin.

She turned to face him and let the dress drop, exposing her toned body and black lace lingerie and stockings. She climbed onto the bed. Danny removed the rest of his clothes and lay next to her. Their hands explored each other. Trisha slid out of her underwear and climbed on top of him. They moved in tune with each other, the intensity rising until a climactic end left them lying breathlessly in each other's arms.

───

Danny woke in the morning to Trisha's wandering hands and soft lips on his neck. They made love again, this time slower and with more purpose, then showered and breakfasted. At eight o'clock, Danny drove her to Greenwood Security and kissed her goodbye.

───

They went out again a couple of days later; this time for a pizza and a movie. This, rather than the posh restaurant, was more Danny's style. He felt at ease and relaxed and ended up in her bed once more.

He drove her into work again. Pulling up outside the office block, she gave him a lingering kiss and gorgeous smile before disappearing into the building.

The minute she was out of sight he wanted to see her again.

CHAPTER 18

Scott had returned from a business trip, so Danny headed over to return his car. Forty minutes later he drove into the underground car park and carefully reversed into the designated bay. He walked towards the stairwell door, stopping to rummage through his pockets for Scott's keys and entrance fob. A movement out of the corner of his eye made him glance left. A short, slim guy with small, round glasses, dressed in a blue boiler suit and baseball cap climbed into the passenger seat of a white Transit van on the far side of the car park. Danny turned back to the door and tapped the fob on the security pad. The lock buzzed open. He pulled on the door and glanced back in the van's direction. A second man, dressed like the first, appeared from the far side of the van and opened one of the rear doors. He threw a bag in and slammed it shut, then disappeared back around the van. Danny had seen the guy's back for only a few seconds but had noticed his build— tall, wide and square, with a neck like a tree trunk. A definite muscle freak. There was something about the man's physique and the way he moved... it triggered the spark of a memory from a long time ago. Shaking it off, he walked through the door and started up the stairs. His phone rang in his pocket, pushing the nagging sensation away. He pulled it out.

'Hi, Paul. What's up?'

'There's been a development regarding Scott's friend.'

'Don't tell me—Scott's overactive imagination,' said Danny cheerily.

'I'm afraid not. They found Amaya Sato and her boyfriend murdered yesterday. I have some friends at MI6 who'd like to have a chat with you and Scott.'

'Wait, *what?* MI6? Amaya's dead? How?'

'Looks like a gang hit. Drugs and money all over the place. The boyfriend and his

cousin were murdered by machine-gun fire. Amaya was raped and beaten before they broke her neck. Too much of a coincidence for my—'

'Shit. Nicholas Snipe.'

Danny hung up and hurtled up the stairs three at a time. As he approached the landing, he slowed and moved silently to the side of the apartment door. After gently sliding the key into the Yale lock, he flicked it with the quietest of clicks and opened the door just a crack. Keeping his body to the side, he moved his head near the opening and listened. All was quiet. No music, no TV, no bullets whizzing. Scott never had the apartment quiet. He liked noise even when he worked. The stench of gas filled Danny's nostrils and drove him to action. He went into the hall and then the lounge, eyes scanning all the way. Scott was on the sofa, bloody and beaten. His left foot was pointing at an unnatural angle, showing the leg had been broken at the shin. For a second Danny thought he was dead. Then he saw Scott's chest moving slowly as he breathed. He quickly checked the rest of the rooms in the apartment to make sure no one else was there, before spotting Scott's mobile on the kitchen worktop. Out of the headphone socket hung a matchbox-sized unit with two bare wires coming out of the top. A simple detonator.

'Shit, shit.'

He ran to Scott, grabbed him by the waist, and hoisted him over his shoulder. The movement forced a groan from Scott's semi-conscious body. Danny's head spun from the gas, but he pushed himself to the limit and ran for the front door. He lowered Scott to the floor and worked the double lock to open it. Then he placed his forearms under Scott's armpits dragged him backwards onto the landing. Scott's mobile rang. The boom of the explosion came only a fraction of a second later. The shockwave blew them both across the landing and into the door of the apartment opposite, their combined weight shattering it inwards. Danny lay on the carpet, Scott unconscious on top of him. He sucked air into his winded chest and glanced across to the living room. Concussed and with ears ringing, he tried to make sense of the vision before him. Scott's neighbour, Mr Chilvers, stood dumbfounded, dressed in a blond wig, lingerie, stockings, and high heels. Danny dragged himself from under Scott, checked his friend was still breathing, and got to his feet.

'Call an ambulance,' said Danny, pointing at Scott. 'And for God's sake, put some fucking clothes on.'

Mr Chilvers nodded, embarrassed and speechless, and reached for the phone. Danny ran through the door and glanced at the sea of destruction, smoke and flames in Scott's apartment. Ignoring the pain in his head and ribs, he descended the stairs at a furious pace, leaping almost a flight at a time. The men in the van would hang around for visual confirmation that the apartment had gone up. He thumped the exit button and charged through to the underground car park. On the other side, he halted and did a quick three-sixty to assess the situation, his training kicking in. The exit gate at the far end of the car park had clicked shut and he could just make out a Transit van pulling off beyond it. He ran to Scott's car and leapt in. It started with a roar. He sped towards the exit barrier, changing down a gear and kicking the throttle. The car smashed through the barrier in an explosion of plastic as he roared up the ramp to the street above. The van was out of sight, so he tore along the few hundred metres to the main road at the bottom of the street. He stopped, looked left and right. No sign of the van in the moving traffic. He took a guess—the van would probably head out of town—and turned right, away from the city centre. Using all the power of the 3-litre, 425bhp engine, he drove manically along the crowded London street, overtaking around bollards and undertaking in the bus lanes. His guesswork was rewarded as he caught a glimpse of the van five cars ahead. *Bloody Snipe.* Over a decade ago, a smaller and younger version of the man had passed SAS selection and been assigned to Danny's Alpha team. After the third mission, concerns were raised. Snipe, it transpired, was a sadistic bastard who took pleasure in killing and torturing. Snipe's resentment of Danny as team leader had also become an issue; he frequently took his own initiative instead of following orders. The situation came to a head when they were combing a village for a high-ranking Al Qaeda member. Snipe peeled off from the team as they searched a building for their target. With no response on comms and fearing the worst, they entered a neighbouring house to catch up with him. While performing a sweep, they found a villager with his throat cut. In another room they found Snipe over the man's wife. He'd raped and beaten her before snapping her neck.

'Al Qaeda fucker,' was all Snipe had said as he grabbed his kit and walked out.

Outside, Danny had launched himself at Snipe, punching him full in the face. The blow had broken his nose. It had taken the other three members of the team to stop the two of them killing each other. The team had reported Snipe, but it was a sensitive time for bad press, and Snipe swore blind that the villager had killed the woman before attacking him: he'd killed in self-defence. They dropped the case, and they reassigned Snipe. But before he left, he promised retribution on every member of the Alpha squad. Not long after, they discharged him for failing his psychological evaluation. Danny slowed to match the traffic and followed well back. The van headed north and turned onto the A12. Danny didn't let it out of his sight.

CHAPTER 19

The protective sheath of adrenaline was wearing off, letting in the pain. Danny did a quick assessment while he drove. His left shoulder and ribs hurt, and his head was banged up, but other than that everything seemed to move okay. His ears were still ringing, but not as much as earlier, and he could feel blood trickling down his forehead from a cut on top of his head, but all in all he wasn't in too bad a shape. The van indicated and turned off towards Stratford. He followed several cars back. The indicator flicked on again. It seemed they were heading for CMS. As he reached the junction, he heard the sirens. In the rear-view mirror blue lights flashed up fast behind him.

'No fucking way. Not now.'

He pulled over, not wanting to alert the van to a police escort. Anyway, he was confident about where they were going. Now he just had to get rid of these clowns. He got out of the car and walked directly towards the approaching shocked- looking officer. The kid didn't look old enough to get served in a bar. With one hand on the Taser clipped to his belt the officer said, 'Sir, please stay where you are.' He sounded slightly nervous. Danny realised the state he was in, covered in crap, with a singed jumper, burnt hair, and blood trickling down his face.

'Is there a problem, Officer?' he said calmly, and smiled.

'Sir, stay there. This car has been reported as speeding away from an explosion at Kingsway Apartments thirty minutes ago. Please stand facing the car with your hands placed behind your head.' The officer moved slowly towards him while a colleague got out the driver's side of the police car.

Shit, this was taking too long. The driver would have called for backup. He turned slowly to face the car.

I've got to get out of here now if I'm going to catch that van.

He ran through his options. The officer approached. Danny didn't relish what had to come next. The officer was behind him now, handcuffs out and ready. Danny dropped to one knee fast and powered his elbow back and up into the young policeman's groin. Keeping his momentum, he spun around and dealt two measured blows to pressure points on the officer's neck and temples, putting him out cold. The second officer had been caught off guard by the speed of the attack and was fumbling with his Taser. Danny closed in on him. The officer freed the charged Taser and pointed it forwards just as Danny grabbed his wrists and twisted them downwards. He pulled on top of the officer's trigger finger, firing the Taser into the man's thigh. Danny released his wrists and jumped back just as fifty thousand volts coursed through the floored police officer. Although he'd taken out the policemen in less than thirty seconds, passing cars were already stopping. Nervous drivers unsure of what to do just stared. On the pavement behind the police car, a group of teenagers were doing what comes naturally—filming with their phones.

Great. I'll be a YouTube sensation by teatime.

Hearing more sirens in the distance, he ran to his car, jumped in and jammed it into first. Throttle down, the powerful car took off in a cloud of smoking rubber.

Danny covered the three miles to the industrial park in under two minutes before breaking sharply to a crawl as he approached the CMS building. He pulled up to the kerb opposite and surveyed the building. The Transit was parked by the rear loading bay doors. Other than that, the place looked deserted. He got out of the car and walked around to the boot. Then he opened it without taking his eyes off the building. He lifted the board that covered the spare tyre compartment and pulled out the tool roll. After removing the tyre brace, he threw the rest back in and shut the boot. Then he was back behind the wheel, the tyre brace on the passenger seat. He backed up along the street, stopping some fifty metres away, then calmly clicked his seat belt in and pulled it tight. Gripping the steering wheel with both hands, he dropped the clutch and punched the accelerator. Smoke poured off the tyres as they fought for grip. The car careened towards the entrance of CMS, and still gaining speed, tore through the twin sliding doors with a metallic screech and a shower of shattered glass. The airbags deployed on impact and Danny was deafened for the second time that day. He kicked the twisted door open, grabbed the tyre brace and stepped out into the reception area, his expression like granite. No voices, no sound of approaching footsteps. He looked through the observation window into the server room. Nothing. He turned away.

Wait

He turned back. Every fourth or fifth cabinet was

dotted with a magnetic explosive device with small, red, synchronised timers.

Shit.

They were covering their tracks. His mind raced. Time was short. He moved hastily up the stairs, scanning carefully as he went through the deserted offices towards the back of the building. He spotted two more devices taped to the concrete uprights supporting the ceiling, but there was no sign of Snipe or the other man. As he neared the back of the building, he glanced out the window. The Transit van was directly below him. He turned back to the office. The smaller man with glasses was hurrying up the corridor towards him. Danny dropped below a partition wall, listening to the footsteps fast approaching. He breathed slowly to calm himself. When the footsteps were close enough, he sprung up and planted the tyre brace in the man's face. His glasses broke in two and the cartilage in his nose collapsed. The blow took him clean off his feet and landed him out cold. Danny checked he hadn't killed the guy, then zipped to the end of the building in pursuit of Snipe. He did a sweep of the remaining six rooms. With no sign of him, he paused in the last room and took a quick look at the explosive device taped to the pillar. He picked at the corner with his fingernail and peeled away the tape over the timer, revealing the digital display.

'Oh, you've gotta be fucking kidding me.' The small red clock counted down to fifty-nine seconds. He sprinted down the corridor, leapt over the unconscious man, and hammered the tyre brace into the window. The inner pane shattered into thousands of tiny pieces, but the second pane was still intact. With the clock in his head still counting down, Danny hammered it until it eventually splintered and gave way. He grabbed the unconscious guy and slung him over his shoulder, then threw him out the window and onto the Transit van roof. Still counting seconds, he climbed onto the sill and jumped out after him. He landed with a metallic boom on the roof, grabbed the guy's ankle, and slid forward. They lurched over the front, over the bonnet and onto the floor. Danny hunkered down and covered his ears with his hands. The devices exploded in unison. The sound was huge. Glass shards rained down in all directions as every window in the building exploded outwards. The loading bay doors blew off their hinges and clanged into the back of the van. A searing heatwave followed, curling round the front of the van. Danny felt a burning sensation at his ankles as the flames pushed underneath the van, then the backdraft sucked them back as fast as they'd come. He removed his hands from his ears. Over the roar of flames and the screech of collapsing metal behind him, he heard multiple sirens and an approaching helicopter from in front. A result of his attack on the two police officers or for the explosion? He couldn't be sure. Either way, this was going take a lot of explaining. The man next to him stirred, groaning and reaching for his face. For no other reason than he felt like it, Danny punched him hard in the side of the face, putting him on the floor again. Seconds later, police cars poured into the car park, fanned out and screeched to a halt. Armed officers assumed defensive positions all round them.

'Armed police! Kneel down with your hands behind your head!' They relayed the instructions through a loud-hailer from the hovering helicopter overhead.

Danny did as he was told. Within seconds, he was swamped, cuffed and thrown into the back of a police transport van.

CHAPTER 20

Still in handcuffs, the police medic checked Danny over. She cleaned him up and applied butterfly strips to the gash on his head. Then he was escorted roughly to the holding cells by the custody sergeant. His watch, wedding ring and personal items were bagged before fingerprints and mug shots were taken. The sergeant offered him his phone call, and they showed him to a cubicle with an unbreakable-looking plastic phone screwed firmly to the wall. He called Paul.

There was a click and Trisha answered.

'Greenwood Security. How can I help you?'

'Trish, it's Danny. Sorry, I haven't got long. I need to talk to Paul urgently.'

'Are you okay? You're not hurt, are you? From the explosion, I mean.' Danny could hear the tremble in her voice.

'No, no, I'm fine, honest. Just a few scrapes and bruises. But how did you know?'

'This is Paul we're talking about. He's not here but said you'd ring. He said sit tight and say nothing. Someone will be with you soon.' She sounded a little more together now.

'Err, okay.'

The police officer next to him told him to finish up.

'I've got to go, Trish. I may be a little late for our dinner date,' he said with a tired chuckle. 'Call me.'

'I will. Got to go.'

The officer muttered to himself as he hauled Danny along the beige-painted corridor with its shiny vinyl flooring and strong smell of bleach. He didn't take much notice. His taking out two officers probably hadn't helped much with police relations. With a push to the left, the officer showed him into a cell and uncuffed him. He backed out the door and slammed it shut. Instead of being intimidated, Danny was glad of the quiet. He'd been held in places that made this look like a holiday camp. Lying down on the hard, plastic bench-come-bed, he closed his eyes and breathed deeply. His body ached and the last remnants of adrenaline had gone. Exhaustion took over and he drifted into a deep sleep.

The metallic clang of the door being opened forced him from asleep to fully awake in the blink of an eye—operational habits again: be alert or be dead. He sat upright despite bitter complaints from his ribs and shoulder. Two officers entered the cell.

'Up and face the wall with your hands behind you,' said the larger of the two men.

Danny stood slowly and tensed for a second as his eyes locked with theirs. Then he turned and placed his hands behind his back. He sensed the two men hesitating before approaching and guessed the news of his assault had spread through the station like wildfire. Right now, he was likely as popular as a fart in an astronaut's suit. They cuffed him roughly and pushed him towards the door.

'Interview room five, please,' said a middle-aged man in a cheap, crumpled, grey suit, standing at the far end of the corridor.

They escorted him into the room, dumped him in a chair, and removed his cuffs. They left, replaced by the crumpled guy and a woman in a pristine navy blue trouser suit. They sat opposite him, trying their level best to keep eye contact as he trained his gaze from one to the other.

Grey Suit pressed the record button and spoke.

'Interview with Mr Daniel Pearson commencing at 6.30 p.m., 4th May 2017. Present are DI Helen Piper and DCI Greg Mallory.'

Mallory opened a file in front of him and continued. 'Mr Pearson, you are being interviewed today to establish your involvement with the explosions at—'

'My involvement amounts to getting blown up... twice,' said Danny.

'I'm asking the questions here, Mr Pearson,' said Mallory, the irritation clearly visible on his face. 'We have you fleeing the scene of an explosion at high speed in a car that doesn't belong to you. Also assaulting two police officers and evading arrest. You then assaulted a CMS employee, Mr Downing, right before that building was also destroyed in an explosion. A rather eventful day, don't you agree?' Mallory finished his speech and looked rather pleased with his theatrical summary.

Danny was about to answer when the door swung open and a man entered in a sharp charcoal-coloured suit. He was tall with short blond hair that sported a razor-straight parting to the right and a neatly combed-over fringe.

'Edward Jenkins, MI6,' he said. He leant over the table, stopped the recording, and pressed the delete button.

'What the hell do you think you're doing?' said Mallory, rising from his seat.

'Mr Pearson is working with us on matters of national security,' said Edward calmly, and handed some paperwork to Mallory.

'Ready to go, Mr Pearson?' Edward turned back to Mallory. 'Any discussion regarding Mr Pearson, Mr Downing, or today's events will be viewed as a breach of the Official Secrets Act. Do I make myself clear?' Edward turned and smiled at Danny. 'Paul Greenwood sends his regards.'

Danny stood up and the red-faced DCI threw the paperwork on the table.

'He's suspected of a murder, terrorism and the assault of two police officers. You can't just take him,' said Mallory, moving to block the door.

'Hmm, if you don't want to be back on traffic duty for the foreseeable future, I suggest you move out the way.' Edward spoke calmly and confidently, leaving them with no doubt he had the power to carry out his threat.

Conflict was written all over Mallory's face, and though he tried to hold his ground, he soon bottled it and moved out of the way. Danny collected his personal effects from the desk sergeant and Edward led him past more than several furious officers and out of the station. Two black Range Rovers with obscured windows awaited them.

'In you get, old chap. We have a few things to discuss regarding our friend in the car behind.'

Danny glanced over his shoulder and got in the back. Both cars moved off quietly into the London traffic.

CHAPTER 21

Danny relaxed. He trusted Paul with his life so guessed Edward must be okay.

'Where are we going and what did that guy mean by being suspected of a murder?'

'Danny—may I call you Danny?' Edward asked.

'Sure,' Danny said.

'I'm taking you to meet a specially assembled task force. We'd like your assistance with our investigation,' said Edward. His voice was calm, even jovial.

'Oh, and we thought it prudent to tell the press that Mr Miller died in the explosion... just in case his attackers decide to have another go. He's in hospital and stable. One of our team is on guard.'

'Am I still under arrest?'

'Good God, no!' said Edward, smiling.

They sat in silence for the remainder of the drive until they pulled onto the driveway of a large house in Muswell Hill. There was a high wall around the perimeter. Big, electronically-controlled gates closed behind them. Danny followed Edward toward the house and peered back over his shoulder. Two men dressed in casual jeans and sweat-shirts got out of the other car and guided a handcuffed man with a cloth hood over his head out of the back. He assumed it was the supposed CMS employee, Mr Downing. As they passed Danny, one of the men gave him a nod. The other winked. Edward waved him into the kitchen and pulled out a chair.

'Take a seat. Tea, coffee?' he said, popping the kettle on.

'Coffee, white, one sugar,' said Danny.

'Do you like Chinese? One of the lads has gone out for takeaway. Should be back in a minute.' Edward handed him a steaming mug.

'Err, sure,' Danny said.

The kitchen door opened a crack, and a head popped around. 'Boss is here.'

'Thank you, Tom,' said Edward.

Danny heard footsteps coming down the hall. He turned to look just as Paul walked in.

'Coffee, Paul?' said Edward.

'Yes, please,' Paul replied, taking a seat opposite Danny. 'You okay, Danny? Not hurt? Damn good work getting Scott out and tracking down our man upstairs.'

'No, I'm fine. What the hell's going on, Paul?'

'All will be revealed shortly,' Paul said. He turned to Edward. 'What's on the menu tonight, Edward?'

'Chinese. John's gone for it. He'll be back any minute.'

'Good man. Follow me, Danny,' said Paul. Entering the front room, it surprised Danny to find something resem-bling a full- scale incident room. They had fixed three large whiteboards to the far wall which were covered with photographs of faces. Overlapping arrows and scribbled notes linked the images. In front of him stood a row of desks covered in papers, computers and printers. Cables ran all over the place. Three men sat behind the screens, all dressed casually. They worked feverishly, scanning an array of open windows on the monitors. Apart from Edward and Paul, all the other team members were in their mid-twenties with short crewcuts and well built. Definitely military types; they reminded Danny of his old unit.

'Grub's up,' said a guy laden with carrier bags full of plastic tubs of food.

'Grab a plate and we'll have a chat,' said Paul, following John into the kitchen. One of the computer guys got up from his desk. 'You must be the legendary Danny Pearson. I'm Tom. That's Glen. And the ugly one on the end is Simon. John's upstairs looking after our guest.' The other team members nodded. 'It's a pleasure to meet you, mate. One hell of a service record.'

Danny nodded, and they went through to the kitchen. He grabbed a plateful of takeout and a can of lager and wandered back into the front room. He sat with Paul at a beaten-up table near the whiteboards.

'Okay, I'll give you a quick breakdown of what's going on.' Paul took a couple of large mouthfuls and a swig of lager. 'Around eighteen months ago, Edward's mob intercepted communication messages between a key member of an extremist group calling themselves The Faith, Akbar Bakr in Syria, and a London mosque preacher called Barzan Naser. The mosque has been under surveillance after complaints about extremist grooming from concerned parents.'

'Is Barzan Naser related to the Kadah Naser I met at CMS?' said Danny.

'Sharp as ever—yes, Kadah is Barzan's nephew. Now going back to the intercepted messages... there was talk of an attack, some sort of a great and glorious program to bring us all to our knees and cripple the country, blah,

blah. Usual stuff. These guys talk in riddles and are always bringing someone to their knees.'

Paul stood and walked over to the whiteboards and pointed at the images as he ran through the key facts. 'That's Amaya Sato, poor girl. Tortured, raped and then had her neck snapped. On the surface it looked like a Yakuza revenge hit for her boyfriend and his cousin's dealing behind their backs.'

'Nicholas Snipe.'

'Yes, you said that on the phone before the explosion at Scott's, so I pulled his file. Nasty bastard, isn't he?' Paul pointed to an old service photo of Snipe.

'He was at Scott's with the guy upstairs,' said Danny.

'Ah.' Paul tapped an image. 'Came in about an hour ago. Robert Smith. Former Australian SAS regiment. Specialist in surveillance and explosives.' He indicated the two CCTV images. One showed a tall, lean, athletic man in partial side profile. A baseball cap covered mid-length wavy brown hair and wrap-around shades. The other photo offered a side profile of a shorter, stockier man with a deep scar from his right brow to the centre of his cheek. He looked Indian or maybe Mexican.

'We're fairly sure these two are part of a four-man hit team with Snipe and Smith. We don't know who they are yet, and it'd be nice if Mr Smith helped us fill in some blanks. Unfortunately, he's smart and knows we don't have much on him, so he'll probably tough it out.'

Paul moved across to pictures of Amaya and four other faces. More arrows and notes criss-crossed the images.

'These people were programmers. According to friends and family, all had been developing programs for CMS for the past one to two years. Now they're all dead, apparently as a result of unrelated accidents. New York, hit by a truck. Paris, suspected suicide. Berlin, mugged and stabbed.

Sydney, slipped in the shower. And then, of course, Amaya... which brings me to Marcus Tenby,' said Paul.

He tapped a picture of an immaculately groomed Middle Eastern man in his mid- thirties. Arrows pointed to Naser and Barzan on one side and Chris Mayhew and his wife and children on the other. Danny looked closely at the picture of Mayhew.

'Mayhew was the former owner and director of CMS. We think they killed his wife and children, then forced him to sign over the company before disposing of him. There's been no sign of him for months.' Paul moved back to the photo of Amaya. 'I believe Amaya's contacting Scott forced them to accelerate their plans. Killing her to cover their tracks, I can understand, but taking out Scott seems an unnecessary risk... unless they didn't get the program from Amaya and had to get it from Scott. I presume getting that program and the increased interest from you and Scott prompted them to blow up CMS and go to ground. I also think it indicates that they're close to their goal.' Paul stood back and scanned the boards. 'Whatever they've got planned, it's big—a cyber attack of some kind —and it's going to happen soon.'

'Any idea where they've gone?' said Danny.

'Not yet. We're watching Barzan and the mosque in case Kadah or Tenby show up, which is doubtful. They're too clever for that. I think they're still in London. It's a lot of work setting up a new base with the internet and server power needed for a large-scale cyber attack. This means going backwards and forwards from CMS. It would make sense not to travel too far.'

'What do you know about Tenby?' Danny asked.

'Until a month ago, not much, other than Marcus Tenby isn't his real name. Then we dug up an old university photo of Kadah with his classmates, one of whom looked remarkably like Tenby. We ran it through facial recognition and got a match. University records told us the rest. He's actually one Yoseph Mosul. Born in Iraq. Son of wealthy businessman Dinesh Mosul and his wife, Shada. Both were killed in an American bombing raid during the Gulf War.'

'A revenge-motivated radical extremist,' said Danny. He suddenly felt exhausted.

Paul seemed to notice. 'That's enough for one day. Tom will take you home.' He patted Danny on the back. 'I'd like you to work with me on this. Time is running short and finding people, among other things, has always been a particular talent of yours.'

Danny looked hard at Paul for a few seconds before giving him a simple nod. 'Tom will pick you up tomorrow morning at nine.'

CHAPTER 22

The morning sun beamed its early rays into the grubby works unit. Rusty roll-down shutters covered the loading bay and the white paint on the wooden entrance door was peeling badly. Built under the railway arches in the 1930s, it had been home to a florist, a cabinet-maker, a builder, and a taxi company over the decades. For the past six years it had been empty and fallen into disrepair. It was tucked away down a quiet potholed side-turning in a part of Stratford untouched by the money thrown at the Olympic Games regeneration. The three gleaming cars—an Audi S4, a Range Rover, and a Mercedes GLE—looked out of place in the overgrown car park. Despite the calm outside, the interior was a hive of activity. Three of Barzan's followers—handpicked for their IT talents—worked at their computers, their fingers dancing over the keyboards at an amazing speed. Several rows of makeshift desks loaded with computer equipment were crammed into any area of free space. Cables and extension leads snaked across the floor to the rear of the unit where three large servers stood. Each had its own ultra-fast fibre link to the internet. Cooling fans whirred and data lights danced, casting a green and orange flickering pattern across the wall.

Kadah sat next to Shan. Marcus moved between three machines, watching streams of code scrolling across the monitors.

'Status report.'

'Another hour,' said one of the young men.

'Just finishing. Ten minutes,' said another.

'An hour and a half, possibly two hours,' said the last one with a slightly shaky voice.

'Kadah?' Marcus shouted, his face still on the screens.

'Just finishing the patch programs now. Half-hour at most,' Kadah said calmly.

'Good, good. Shan, how is the firewall access coming?'

'It is all ready, Marcus.'

They worked on silently, the tapping of keyboards and hum of cooling fans the only sound.

They froze in unison at the sound of a vehicle crunching its approach on gravel outside. Everyone stared at the shutters, as if they might see through at their visitors. Barzan picked up an Uzi and went to the front door while Kadah and Marcus pulled out their handguns.

Barzan looked through the spyhole and signalled for them to lower their guns. 'It is only Peters and his men.'

He slid the large metal deadbolt back and Snipe's huge frame pushed through, blocking the view to the outside.

'Steady on, Abdul. You might hurt yourself with that,' he said, pushing past him.

Peters walked in next, followed by Ramirez, who scanned the area before entering and closing the door.

'You're one member short, Mr Peters,' said Marcus while the others went back to their work.

'Smith's detention is of no concern to you. We all know the risks involved,' Peters spoke calmly.

'Can Mr Smith be trusted to keep silent?' Marcus said, barely covering his annoyance.

'Without question. Apart from his being at CMS, there's no solid evidence of him committing any crime.'

'Why has he not been released then?' said Marcus.

'Because of the explosions they'll hold him under the Terrorism Act. They have forty-eight hours before he has the right to a solicitor. Smith was very careful: plastic detonators on plastic explosives—all burnt up. They have no evidence. Our solicitor is already working on getting him out,' said Peters.

'Did Smith make the item I requested before his arrest?' said Marcus, the subject of Smith no longer of interest.

'Yes, Rami has it,' said Peters, waving him to approach the table.

Ramirez pulled a small black box from his jacket pocket. Other than one rubber button on the side, there were no other features.

'Once you press the button, the battery will keep the unit armed for about six days. It's paired to your laptop, as requested, and won't show up on any airport metal detector,' said Ramirez.

'How close does it need to be?' Marcus said, turning the device over in his hand.

'It's very high-grade plastic. I would expect it to kill anyone within a ten-metre radius,' said Peters.

Listening from behind, Kadah and Barzan looked at each other in surprise. This was not something Marcus had discussed with them.

'I have another job for you,' said Marcus, beckoning

Peters, Ramirez and Snipe. Snipe didn't move. 'You! Come here when I tell you.'

A flash of rage burned in Snipe's eyes, and his fingers twitched by his side as he fought the desire to draw his Sig from its shoulder holster and shoot every one of them. Seconds passed. His eyes dulled and he followed the other two men.

'Scott Miller came to CMS accompanied by a man called Rodger Freeman,' said Marcus, tapping at his keyboard. A Facebook page opened, displaying a thirty-second video clip of a man taking down two police officers before tearing away in a blue BMW. The other screen showed CMS CCTV footage of the same blue BMW driving across the car park before crashing through the reception doors.

Marcus tapped a few keys, and a video appeared showing the side of the building. The window above the white Transit van exploded outwards. A second or so later, Smith's limp body was thrown onto the van's roof. Then the man from the Facebook footage dragged Smith down the front of the van. A flash killed the camera feed, and the screen turned to white noise.

'That is Rodger Freeman,' said Marcus, gesturing angrily at the monitors.

'Bollocks. That wanker is Danny Pearson, and he's a fucking big problem,' said Snipe.

Everyone turned to face him.

'He's ex-SAS, and a highly decorated fucker. Hard as a coffin nail.'

'I'll double the price. Find him. I want him dead,' said Marcus, turning back to his computers and gesturing for them to leave.

'No,' Peters said.

Marcus looked up, anger burning in his eyes.

'We've extended our contract too many times and, along with Smith, one or more of our identities might already be compromised. We have completed your contracts. We're done,' said Peters, gently putting his hand on the gun inside his coat. He backed away towards the door, his eyes darting from Barzan to Kadah to Marcus. 'Get the door, Ramirez. Snipe, it's time to go.'

He was within a couple of metres of the door. Marcus, Kadah and Barzan stared at him with cold, dark, unblinking eyes.

Peters arched suddenly backwards, and his mouth opened in a silent scream. Panic and terror filled his eyes before he slumped lifelessly to the ground.

Snipe pulled a large, serrated commando knife from between Peters' shoulder blades.

A grin spread across his face and a hint of insanity glinted in his eyes as he crouched and wiped his knife on Peters' jacket. Then he took the dead man's gun from his coat and tucked it into his own jacket.

Snipe stared at the shocked room. 'Double money upfront—me and Rami.' He looked at Ramirez, who nodded. 'We'll take care of Danny Pearson. I've got unfinished business to settle.'

Marcus waved everyone back to work and, his composure regained, turned to Snipe. 'Half now, half when it's done.'

Snipe didn't move for an uncomfortable few seconds, then he nodded.

'Where would you like your money sent, my friend?'

CHAPTER 23

Daylight crept around the curtain edges. Danny rolled over to look at his watch on the bedside table. The pleasant sensation of having had a restful sleep was quickly a memory as his chest and shoulders screamed their objection to his movement. He sat up gingerly and edged to the side of the bed. His ribs were just as unhappy. He glanced at the full-length mirror in the room's corner; black and purple bruises stared back at him.

'You wanna see the other guy.'

He stretched cautiously and followed a hot shower with a shave. Feeling a lot better, he dressed and headed downstairs.

'Morning, Rob,' he said, drawing out a chair at the kitchen table.

'Fuck me, you look like shit,' said Rob, clicking on the kettle.

'Thanks, love you too,' he replied, sitting down stiffly and nodding as Rob shook a coffee cup at him.

He gave Rob a heavily edited version of the previous

night's events, leaving out everything other than a gas explosion at Scott's apartment.

'You going to see Scott this morning? He had his leg pinned and plastered last night so he should be up for a visit.'

'Sorry, I can't. Tell him I'll get up as soon as I can.' Danny sipped his coffee and checked his watch.

'What are you up to then?' said Rob.

'It's complicated. A job for Paul is the simplest answer.' Danny frowned at the thought of Snipe, Tenby and their killer goons.

Rob's face fell. 'You're going away again?'

'No, this is local. I can't say much but it's to do with Scott and CMS and the program his Japanese friend sent him,' Danny said.

The doorbell saved him from the raft of questions he knew Rob was about to ask. 'Oh, one more thing—don't mention Scott to anyone. Tell Tina too. There'll be an armed guard on Scott's room. I'll let him know you're coming.'

Rob stared at him, dumbfounded. 'Err, armed what?'

'I'll explain more later,' Danny said. He stood painfully and headed for the door. Tom was out front with the black Range Rover.

'Morning, Danny. You look like shit,' said Tom, chuckling as he turned and headed for the car.

'You should see the other guy.'

Danny spent most of the morning getting to know the team. They had moved Smith to MI6 headquarters for questioning, but they doubted they'd get anything out of him. He knew they could keep him for only forty-eight hours without giving him access to legal representation, and with no real evidence, a solicitor would demand his immediate release. Danny took his time running through the information on the boards. He studied the characters in play and the victims and how they'd died. On the table lay Smith's personal effects sealed in clear evidence bags— a wallet, some cash, chewing gum, a watch, and a driving licence with Smith's picture on. It was under the name Arnold Garmen. The back of his mobile phone had been taken off and the SIM card removed. It was plugged into a small box connected to a laptop running some sort of cell-history program.

'Tom, what do we know about Snipe and Co.'s travel arrangements?'

'Err, hang on... I've got it here somewhere,' he said as Danny moved behind him. 'Here we are. We found a link between CMS and an aviation charter company. Nine of the destinations and dates tie in with the deceased cases on the boards,' said Tom, pointing at the monitor.

'What about immigration and CCTV? Don't we have any matches?'

'The fuzzy pictures on the board are from Tokyo—not much help. They flew in on small private jets and used a selection of private commercial airstrips with limited passport control. I have a list of passport names linked to the charter flights—all false IDs.' Tom brought up the list of names and the destinations they'd been used on.

'That's a lot of false ID, and judging by the quality of that driving licence, very expensive. Do we have any leads?' Danny picked up the licence and studied it.

'The licence is genuine apart from the picture. I'm guessing the passports are the same. More a case of identity theft than forgery. No chance of flagging up at immigration that way.'

99

Danny nodded, studying the lists over Tom's shoulder.

Danny frowned. 'They flew back to London every time.'

'Err, yep. Return flight. So?'

'A team like that plans every detail, right? That's why there's no trace. In and out like ghosts,' Danny said. Tom looked puzzled. 'They would have gone straight from one hit to the next and the next. But they had to come back to London for a reason, yes? They wouldn't risk going to the next hit without new passports and IDs. The longer they keep the same identities, the higher the risk of being compromised, and if that happened, they would be arrested at passport control. Their fixer is here in London and, chances are, he fixed more than just IDs. Maybe guns, explosives, information. If we're lucky, he'll have fixed stuff for Tenby, too. And if so, he probably knows where Tenby is or at least how to get hold of him.'

Tom nodded. 'Makes sense. But how do we find him?'

Danny smiled. 'We talk to someone who might have used his services. And I know just the man.'

CHAPTER 24

I n the heart of London, Phillip Gotts sat behind his desk on the second floor of T.A. Leamings, London's oldest privately run bank. Polished oak panels surrounded the room, and centuries-old white-painted sash windows offered views of the Thames all the way to the Houses of Parliament.

Gotts placed his china cup of tea on a coaster so as not to mark the antique walnut desk, or its green leather inlay. Apart from the phones and computer, the office had remained unchanged for over a century and he wouldn't have had it any other way.

He trawled through his emails and flicked through various pieces of paperwork, signing those that demanded his authorisation.

The phone chirruped, breaking his flow. He let it ring a few times before answering it; he thought it emphasised his authority when he kept staff waiting a moment or two.

He looked at the internal extension. Ian Wellan. 'Yes, Ian.'

'Mr Gotts, err, sorry to disturb you, sir. We have a

problem with the computer system. Some accounts seem to have disappeared.'

'Well, have you been on to the tech guys?' asked Gotts, annoyed at being bothered with such trivial matters.

'Yes, sir. I'm waiting for them to get back to… oh, another account's gone, and another.' Wellan's voice sounded a little panicky.

The phone's incoming line flashed.

'I've got MSI on the other line. I'll call you back.' He hung up and tapped the incoming call. 'Phillip Gotts.'

'Mr Gotts, it's Carl Tripp from MSI. I have to shut your systems down and start running backups, I'm afraid. We think you're being hacked and need to run the tracers.'

'Christ, do it, man!' Gotts hung up and headed down to Wellan on the counter floor.

Carl Tripp ran through the protocols for a system breach. He entered the command to shut down the Leamings' system before running the backup and restore. Things started off fine; the system closed, and the backup systems began loading just as they should have. His colleague ran a detection program to find the hacker's IP address and location for the police reports that invariably would have to be filed.

Tripp picked up his phone and pressed the extension for his manager.

'Dom, we've just had a hack attempt at T.A. Leamings. I've shut it down and started running backups and a tracking program.'

'Okay, thanks, Carl. I'll put a call into the cybercrime squad. How long before they're back up and running?'

'Let's see… about twenty minutes. I—hang on, whoa! Dom get down here, please. Now!'

'On my way.'

Tripp had grabbed three more technicians, and all were working furiously at their stations when Dominic arrived.

'What's the problem, Carl?'

'I can't shut Leamings down. Money and accounts are transferring all over the place and it's going across to the backups,' said Tripp. He got up and ran across to his co-workers.

'Have you isolated the mainframe?' said Dominic. 'Shit, Carl. Where is the money being transferred to?' he said, jumping on another workstation.

'Everywhere, nowhere. I can't tell. It's going through everything. Moving and deleting all the data, firewalls, antivirus, hack software… I can't stop it,' said Tripp, frantically tapping the keyboard.

'Pull the plug. Cut the outside line,' Dominic screeched above the growing murmur as more employees wandered over.

'We're losing the secondary backups,' yelled another technician over the din.

'Do something! Someone do something,' Dominic pleaded in the background.

'This can't be happening. We've—'

Fifty monitors crashed a sea of hung screens and critical-error messages. An eerie hush fell across the room. Blank puzzled faces looked at each other with no idea what to do next.

Dominic stood wide-eyed. His mobile rang and he jumped. He pulled it out of his pocket and looked at the caller ID. Dominic's boss, the MD, Stephen Price, glowed back at him.

'Shit.'

———

Gotts now faced the embarrassing task of shutting the bank while they restored the systems. The millionaires and billionaires who banked with Leamings were not the kind of people who would understand a system's failure. His face flushed with anger and frustration. The phones were already ringing—outraged customers demanding service. The staff were patiently fending off questions about why online banking wasn't working and why the phone app had frozen. A wealthy widow was threatening to sue after they had declined her card at Harrods.

'Ian, get on the phone to MSI and find out what the hell's taking so long,' he barked.

'Yes, sir,' said Wellan.

Gotts could hear more phones ringing in the background. Then his monitor froze in front of him.

'Somebody tell me what the hell is going on! Wellan, have you got MSI on the line?'

'Mr Gotts, they said it's all gone,' said Wellan.

'What do you mean, gone?' Gotts shouted.

'Everything—money, accounts, data, backups. All of it.'

Gotts's face went ghostly white.

'The offshore accounts. Tell me we still have the offshore accounts.'

Wellan lowered the phone, slowly shaking his head.

CHAPTER 25

The Range Rover made a detour and pulled into King's College Hospital. The woman at reception gave Danny directions, and he set off up the stairs and along the white corridors. Scott was in a private room under the name Derick Grey for his protection. They had assigned one of his new team members, John Cummings, to today's guard duty. Danny had a quick chat with him. All had been quiet. The only visitors were the odd nurse and Rob, who'd left half an hour earlier. Danny opened the door softly and he found Scott sitting up in bed, working away on a laptop.

'My God, you look worse than I do, old chap,' said Scott. That wasn't strictly true. Scott's face was a mess of black and purple. The beating with a knuckle-dustered fist had left him with numerous cuts, now neatly held together with butterfly stitches. Danny knew that Scott's torso would look much the same. He'd been told by the doctor that Scott had two cracked ribs, besides his freshly plastered leg.

Danny laughed. 'What, with my good looks?'

'I'll be out in the morning. A few weeks' rest and I'll be as good as new,' said Scott.

'Where are you going to stay, mate? I'm sure we could squeeze you in at Rob's.'

'No need, and Rob already offered. I have another apartment in the same block. It's on the first floor. I let it out to a select few corporate clients from time to time. It's empty at the moment, so I'll move in there until they fix my place.' Scott shuffled his weight and winced.

'Another apartment? I definitely should have tried harder at school,' Danny said, shaking his head.

'I'm rather glad of the things you did learn, my friend, or I wouldn't be lying here now.'

They chatted for a bit then Danny checked his watch.

'Sorry, Scotty boy, gotta go.'

As he got up, his phone rang.

'Danny, it's Paul. Where are you?' There was urgency in Paul's voice. 'Just popped in to see Scott. Why? What's up?'

'There's been a cyberattack at T.A. Leamings bank. It's completely wrecked the system. Destroyed all the account data. I need everyone in.'

Danny looked back at Scott. 'Listen, Paul, computers aren't my thing, and I'm chasing another avenue. You'll just have to trust me on this.' He paused for a moment. 'Talk to Scott. Nobody knows more about banking and security software than him.'

Paul's voice became muffled as he spoke to someone his end, then he came back on the line. 'Okay. Get back when you can. Tell John to give his phone to Scott. I'll call him back in a couple of minutes.'

Paul hung up, and Danny relayed the news. Scott perked up immediately.

CHAPTER 26

Danny headed north towards St John's Wood, his original destination. The houses grew steadily larger the closer he got—rows of large renovated properties with modern glass extensions. The area was home to pop stars, actors, and London's money men. He pulled up outside the largest house on the street. A high rendered wall and solid oak electric gates protected it from intruders. Danny pressed the intercom.

'Yes,' came a gruff, tinny voice.

'I'm here to see Harry.'

'You have an appointment?' said an impatient voice.

'Tell him it's Danny Pearson.'

The intercom clicked, and he stood in silence for a couple of minutes.

'Drive into the courtyard and park on the left,' said the voice as the gates opened inwards.

Danny drove into the courtyard and pulled over to the left. The right-hand side was full of cars and 4x4s, all top-of-the-range Mercedes and Range Rovers. And there was a white Bentley with *HK1* on the registration plate. Four men in black suits lined the front of the house. They had the look of past-their-prime boxers or bare-knuckle fighters: big shoulders, flat noses, slightly overweight, with hard-looking faces. Danny picked out the slight bulge of a gun in a shoulder holster under the left arm of each man. Two of the men approached him.

'Stay there, please. Arms up.'

Danny did as instructed. One man passed a wand over him then the other patted him down. When they were satisfied, they led him inside to a large, modern sitting room. The taller of the two men left. The other stood at the door, doing his best to look hard and intimidating.

'Nice weather we've been having,' Danny said, sitting down.

The man just glared.

'You all right, mate? You look a little constipated,' said Danny, taunting him again.

'You wanna watch your fucking mouth before I give you a slap,' said the man, his face starting to flush.

Danny smiled. 'How rude. I just thought you were about to shit yourself.'

The man's faced turned beetroot as he started towards Danny, fists clenched.

'Jake!' boomed the voice of Harry Knight.

It stopped the man in his tracks.

'Fuck off and cool down. He'd have you eating hospital food without even breaking a sweat.'

Still mad at Danny, Jake stomped out of the room.

'Don't wind 'em up. I've got a hard enough job trying to stop the fuckers doing something stupid without you making it worse,' said Harry.

Danny stood and the two men hugged.

'What brings my favourite nephew over to my side of the city? You look like shit. You in trouble?'

'No, nothing like that, but I do need your help,' said Danny, sitting back down.

'I will if I can, but you picked one hell of a week to ask. I've got someone setting off bombs in my city and some fucking clown at the bank says my offshore account's disappeared.'

The door opened and his daughter, May, came in.

'Danny, it's you. I wondered who'd wound Jake up. He's pacing around the garden like a caged animal.' May hurried over and kissed him on the cheek.

'I haven't seen you for ages. What happened to your face?' she said.

'Oh, this looks worse than it is,' he said. 'And I've been working abroad for a while.'

'May, love, go make me and Danny a pot of tea. We've got a bit of business to discuss.'

Danny waited until May had left before speaking. 'Right, I'll get right to it. The explosions and the trouble at your bank are linked. I assume Leamings was your bank. Anyway, that mess is going to take months to sort out. There's worse to come, Harry. We think Leamings was just a test before a major crippling cyberattack on the entire financial system. We've got terrorists who have been paying mercenaries to kill and cover their tracks. Which brings me to why I'm here. The group has been using a fixer in London for new passports and IDs. I need to find that fixer. He's good—high-quality papers, high-tech explosives and guns are no problem.'

Harry sat quietly for a moment. 'Who are you working with on this?'

'A special MI6 task force,' said Danny.

May came in with the tea. She sensed the gravity of the conversation; she put down the tray, smiled and left.

'You know I can't have any involvement with MI6,' said Harry.

'I have to find these guys, Harry. If they succeed in a full-scale attack, it will ruin the country for decades, and I don't have to tell you what impact that will have on your business. I need to find that fixer. How I get that information stays with me.'

Harry poured the tea. 'Danny, you're my blood and I love ya. Your mother would be proud of how you and Rob turned out. And I owe you for saving May from those bastards. Leave it with me. I'll shake the tree and see what falls out.'

With the serious talk over, they chatted about family. May had recovered pretty well after being kidnapped and tortured. A few years ago, the turf war between the Russian Mafia and Harry had taken a heavy toll. Harry's wife had been murdered in a car bomb and May had been taken by Mafia boss Yuri Volkov. They'd kept her captive in a basement and chopped off three of her fingers. Every couple of days a digit had arrived in a Jiffy bag through the post. Enraged and desperate, Harry had asked for Danny's help. The result had been murder and bloodshed all across London until Danny found May and killed Volkov. It was time to go. Harry promised he'd contact him the moment he found anything out. They hugged and Danny left, but not before giving Jake a wink. Danny drove towards the river and headed back to headquarters.

CHAPTER 27

The control room exploded into a hive of frantic activity as Danny walked back in. The team ran around checking firearms and grabbing protective vests.

'Danny, over here,' Paul beckoned him from the other side of the room.

'What's up?' said Danny.

'Someone just texted Smith's phone,' said Paul, sliding the laptop around.

The package is ready. Need a meet urgently.

'We've tracked the number and signal location to Stratford, and the cellular's still turned on. Tom's heading off now. You go with him, John, Simon and Glen,' Paul said, handing out H&K MP5 sub-machine guns to members of the unit. He fetched a Glock, spare magazines and a shoulder holster and gave them to Danny.

'No heroics, please. Edward has sorted paperwork and ID for you and the firearms. So welcome to MI6,' Paul said, handing Danny his ID and pointing him towards Tom, who was strapping himself into a bulletproof vest.

Three minutes later a Range Rover laden with five armed men raced off, blue lights flashing behind the grills and siren wailing.

———

On the roof of a Stratford tower block, Snipe and Ramirez lay near the edge, dressed in Stannah Lifts engineer overalls. Ramirez stared through the sights of a high-velocity sniper rifle. Beside him, Snipe looked in the same direction through binoculars. Over a thousand metres away, parked on a small patch of wasteland, was the Transit van they'd been driving earlier.

'What do you think?'

'Not sure, Rami.'

'Give it until two o'clock.'

'Yeah, if they're any good they'll have traced the phone and got a location by now. I wanna see who we're up against—plod, special ops or a bunch of suits,' said Snipe.

He pulled up his binoculars and scanned the roads again.

———

Danny sat in the passenger seat next to Tom.

'How far away are we from the phone signal?' Danny asked.

'A couple of miles,' Tom replied.

'Turn off the sirens, Tom. Slow approach.' Danny looked at the three men in the back. 'We'll park up a hundred metres back from the location. Me and Tom will check out the situation and advise over radio.'

The men nodded. Danny fixed his earpiece and did a sound check. A few minutes later they pulled up smoothly outside a small row of shops just down the road from the flagged location on Tom's mobile. Danny and Tom got out, large coats covering their protective vests and firearms. They started walking up the street.

'Hold up. Blacked-out Range Rover at ten o'clock. Two guys are out and moving towards the van. I can't get a good look at them through these, but they look like spooks to me,' said Snipe.

'I've got them. They're nearly at the van. Yep, spooks, plain clothes, padding under coat and bulge under left side. Vests and firearms.' Ramirez shifted the rifle's scope to see their faces. 'Ear piece, right ear of one.' He moved the scope slightly again, so the crosshairs were squarely on the side of the other man's head. 'Holy shit, you'll never guess who's down there.'

'Who?' said Snipe, leaning forward and wishing his binoculars were more powerful.

'Our target, Pearson. Shall I slot him?' Ramirez said, sliding a round into the chamber, never taking his eye from the scope.

'No, not unless we have to. Let the van get them. Save us having to evac quickly.'

'Just around the corner,' said Tom as they passed a newsagent at the end of the row.

Danny peered around the corner. A white Transit van was parked in the middle of a small patch of wasteland. The hairs on the back of his neck stood on end. He had a bad feeling about this.

'Doesn't feel right. It's too easy.'

He inched around the corner towards the van. Tom followed, both tracking with their eyes for any sign of something out of place.

———

'Come on, you stupid bastard. Try the door,' Snipe growled.

Pearson reached the van's back door. Ramirez continued to hold him in his crosshairs. Pearson froze at the door, then turned slowly around and looked straight at the rooftop. Ramirez flinched.

'No way he can see us from this range,' he said, and settled back into his aim.

———

Danny scanned the buildings. For a second he thought he'd seen a flash of reflected sunlight from the top of a tower block, but he couldn't be sure. He locked his gaze and waited. He didn't see it again and turned back to the van.

'Whoa, Tom, don't touch the van. I've been blown up twice in the past week and don't want to make it a hattrick. Call in the bomb squad. This feels all wrong.'

Danny backed away from the vehicle. Tom withdrew his hand from the lock and pulled out his mobile as he followed Danny.

———

'They're moving away from the van,' said Ramirez.

'Fuck. Take him out,' Snipe growled.

Ramirez steadied his breathing and concentrated the

crosshairs on Pearson's forehead, following him as he walked back along the pavement towards the Range Rover. He aimed slightly ahead and above his target, allowing for travel time and bullet drop. He exhaled and gently squeezed the trigger, releasing the bullet on its deadly path with only a pop from the suppressed barrel.

———

It took just under two seconds to travel a thousand metres, the same time required for a motorbike courier to ride directly into the line of sight. The bullet struck the rider through the throat, sending him and his bike into the back of a parked car ten metres in front of Danny and Tom, with a sickening thump. On instinct Danny tackled Tom to the ground and pulled him behind a small van. A fountain of arterial blood pumped upwards from the biker and sprawled across the car roof. It declined as his blood pressure plummeted and the last seconds of life vanished from the gaping wound in his neck. A red mist hung briefly in the air then vanished.

'Sniper fire, sniper fire, due south from our location. We need backup and a police helicopter,' Danny yelled.

'Roger that. What do you want us to do, Danny?' said John in the earpiece.

'Get out of the car kerb-side and stay low until a helicopter's en route. The sniper should be long gone by then.'

Danny glanced forward to see if there was anything he could do for the rider, but the poor sod had bled out.

———

'Fucking twat on a bike,' said Snipe furiously from behind his binoculars.

'Time to go,' said Ramirez.

'Yeah, yeah. Just get me the number plate of that Range Rover through your scope first. We'll see if Hamish can trace it.'

Ramirez moved back, ready to dismantle the gun and make a quick exit.

'Wait, Rami. Let's pop the Claymore first. That'll keep them fuckers busy for a while.' Snipe grinned as Ramirez lay back down, aimed the sniper rifle just below the handle on the van, and slowed his breathing once more.

Danny and Tom remained squatting behind the van. They yelled at the few bystanders along the path to move away and take cover. Further up the street, the rest of the team ensured no one else stumbled into the area.

'You okay, Tom?' Danny said.

'Yeah, I'm—'

A deafening boom was followed by a blast wave as thousands of tiny ball bearings ripped through the wooden fence on the far side of the wasteland and the cars parked directly in front. Danny and Tom were far enough around the corner to avoid the ricocheting shrapnel and the full force of the blast. The noise of aftermath—ingrained from years of active service facing exploding IEDs and land-mines—filled Danny's ears, with injured civilians scream-ing, and car and house alarms wailing. He heard the approaching sirens and the distant whoop of a police helicopter.

'Fuck it. I'm going to help the injured,' said Danny as he left cover and ran to a young woman across the street. She'd been hit in the legs by multiple ball bearings.

In his earpiece he heard Tom calling the rest of the

team to bring the trauma kit from the car and help the wounded while he called for ambulances. Danny put pressure on the woman's legs and glanced over to see what was left of the Transit van. The burning chassis had been stripped from the rear of the van. Only part of driver's cab remained. Most of it was bent forward in strips like a metal banana skin.

'Snipe. Bloody lunatic,' Danny said under his breath.

CHAPTER 28

T he mood under the arches was celebratory. Marcus
and Kadah slapped each other on the back while
Barzan congratulated his three recruits on their
contribution to the cause.

'Where is Shan? He should be here celebrating,' said
Kadah.

'I have him on an errand. He will be back soon,'
Marcus replied.

'I must contact Akbar and tell him the test went well,'
said Barzan heading towards the door and beckoning the
three young men to follow as he went.

'Wait, my brothers. The Faith truly thanks you for your
contribution,' said Marcus, smiling as he moved between
them. 'I'm afraid you have gained too much knowledge of
things that could hurt our mission.'

The three young men looked confused.

'Don't worry, my friends. They will remember you as
martyrs to the cause. Your glory in the afterlife awaits you,'
Marcus said, moving to one side before his words and the
panic could sink in.

118

He picked up a gun from the table and unloaded the entire clip into the startled followers. He turned to Barzan and placed the gun carefully back on the table.

'Go call Akbar. Tell him the attack will take place as planned.'

His eyes dared Barzan to challenge him but none was forthcoming. Barzan had known as well as he that the young followers had to be sacrificed. The man nodded as he backed out the door.

'Kadah, go with Uncle and make sure there is no trace of us at the mosque. I want you and Barzan back here at 11.00 p.m. I will prime the American servers and destroy all the data here. Then, upon your return, we will burn this place to the ground.'

The conversation was over. Time for Kadah and Barzan to leave. As the sound of cars died away, Marcus made a call.

'Where are you, Shan?' he demanded.

'They picked me up as you said, Marcus. They tell me I will be there in fifteen minutes. The road is bumpy, Marcus, and my belly hurts,' Shan's feeble voice replied. 'Be strong, my brother. Just give him the laptop and start the video call as we planned and Allah will reward you. Remember, he's an infidel and a liar, and must be dealt with.' Marcus talked slowly and softly, as a father would to his child.

'Yes, as Allah wills it. I will be there soon.'

'The Faith is with us,' said Marcus and hung up.

He sat at his computer and waited.

Time passed excruciatingly slowly. After forty minutes, doubt crept into Marcus's mind. Was Shan up to the task or had he given the game away? The secure video-call notification broke the tension as it popped up on his monitor. In the middle of the screen was the face of The Faith leader, Akbar Bakr, with two of his generals either side of him.

'Marcus, this man says you wished to tell us in person of your successful attack against our enemies,' said Akbar, smiling.

'Yes, Akbar. Is Shan still there with you?'

'He is here, yes. Tell me, has the money from our enemy been transferred to us yet, and is everything ready to bring the hated Americans to their knees?' Marcus could hear the excitement in his voice.

'No, Akbar. The money is mine and I have many hated enemies. I hated my parents for sending me away to school. I hated the Americans for killing my parents and bombing my homeland. I hate Barzan for twisting my mind and making me a slave to Al Qaeda and The Faith. I hate the English because they despise me. I hate you, Akbar, for making me do your dirty work, and I hate the twisted version of faith you cowards hide behind. It is time, Shan.'

Marcus spoke so calmly that Akbar and his generals could only look blankly at each other, unable to comprehend what he'd just said.

Shan moved into view. He walked up to Akbar as Marcus pressed the command on his keyboard. It activated the device buried in Shan's abdominal cavity. The screen flashed, and the signal was lost.

Marcus turned off his monitor. 'I am sorry, Shan. Your god be with you,' he whispered.

He checked his watch. He had to get to the barber's and change his appearance. Hamish was expecting him and needed a picture for the new passport and ID.

Only then would he be ready for his onward journey and his ultimate goal.

CHAPTER 29

By 6.00 p.m. Danny and the team had finished the debrief with Edward and Paul. The CSI team had established that there'd been a body in the van when it exploded. It would take a couple of days to identify the person as the remains would have filled nothing more than a shoebox. Ballistics had worked out the location of the sniper but found nothing more than an empty shell casing and a couple of boot marks. The finger-print guys were still busy dusting, but Danny knew they wouldn't find anything. In the cab home, he drew strange looks from the driver. Hardly a surprise given he was covered in other people's blood. He walked through Rob's front door to the welcome sound of chatting and laughter. In the kitchen he found Tina cooking while Rob and Trisha chatted at the table. He stood in the doorway, covered in dust, muck and blood. They looked at him and froze.

'It's okay—it's not mine,' he said.

His words barely made a dent in their shock. Trisha

took a minute then walked over and cupped his face in her hands. She gave him a kiss.

'Bad day at the office, honey?'

He smiled and kissed her back. 'Yeah, but it just got a whole lot better.'

Rob and Tina smirked.

'All right, you two, pour me a drink while I jump in the shower and change,' he said, patting Trisha on the bum.

Upstairs in his room, he stripped and moved towards the en-suite bathroom. The ringing phone stopped him mid-track. He contemplated ignoring it until he saw Harry Knight's number flashing.

'Harry,' he said.

'All right, son? I've found out who your fixer is: Hamish Cambell.'

Danny scribbled down the information as Harry relayed it, then hung up and called Paul. He answered on the second ring.

Paul said he'd put the address under surveillance while Edward got the necessary warrants for a raid the following morning. All done, Danny showered, dressed and went downstairs just as Tina was dishing up. After a grilling about the day's events, the conversation took a more relaxed turn. They drank and laughed, and Danny hadn't felt this good for years. Having Trisha there with his brother and future sister-in-law made it all the better. It was late, and with the wine finished they decided to turn in. Danny caught a little smile from Rob as he took Trisha's hand and led her upstairs.

CHAPTER 30

Marcus waited in the old works unit. He'd transformed himself. The once dark, wavy hair had been clipped short and bleached. He was clean-shaven, and dark-rimmed spectacles adorned his face. A plain hooded sweatshirt and cheap jeans had replaced the tailored suit, and an old pair of Adidas trainers finished off the look. Kadah and Barzan entered the unit, and Kadah went for his gun. Marcus spoke quickly to identify himself.

'Brother, the change is incredible. I barely recognise you. Amazing. Do you want us to do the same?' Kadah said, shaking his head in disbelief.

'Give me your gun. I need to torch it along with the unit. We can't take it with us,' Marcus said, extending his hand.

Kadah handed him the weapon. 'You made sure there isn't anything pointing to us at the mosque or house?'

'Yes, Marcus. It is as if we were never there,' said Kadah proudly.

'I couldn't get hold of Akbar, but I will try again later,' Barzan chipped in from behind Kadah.

'No need, Barzan. This is where we part company.' Marcus raised Kadah's gun and picked up his own from the table.

'Marcus, brother, what are you doing?' said Kadah.

'Marcus, I'm your uncle. Put that down,' demanded Barzan.

'You are not my uncle, you fat pig. Kadah, I am sorry,' said Marcus, and emptied the clips into each of them.

He threw the guns down, grabbed a large jerrycan from under the table and poured petrol over the dead bodies, desks and the gas bottles stacked at the rear of the unit. At the door he stood for a moment, then flicked open a Zippo lighter and threw it in. With a whoosh of flame behind him, he climbed into the cheap Toyota he'd bought with cash the day before and headed for the airport.

CHAPTER 31

A nervous Hamish Cambell spotted the Range Rover forty metres down the road. He'd been on edge since spotting a small black car at the end of the street earlier that morning. The sun hadn't come up, and it had been parked discreetly away from the streetlights. Most wouldn't have paid it a second's notice, but Hamish wasn't most people. Sitting motionless in the darkness of his front room, he'd seen the tiny red glow of a cigarette end as the occupant inhaled. It had left an hour ago, and he'd sensed trouble was coming his way. And here it was. Hamish's wiry body exploded into action. His mop of curly copper hair and matching beard swished as he spun. He yanked out the quick-release hard drives from the computers lined on the dining table, then grabbed two mobiles off the kitchen worktop and slung them and the hard drives into a microwave. It bleeped as the timer counted down. The laptop, external hard drives, and a little red notebook went into a sports bag. Glancing down the hall as shadows approached the front door, he jogged through the ground-floor flat. There was no panic, just a well-rehearsed exit

125

plan. He jumped on the bed, opened the window, and climbed out into a walled garden. He moved swiftly towards a small ladder perched against the eight-foot wall at the rear. The buzz of the doorbell coincided with a loud bang as the microwave exploded, followed by the smoke alarm screeching its objection. As he swung his legs over the wall and disappeared, he heard the front door implode. His flat had been well chosen. There were five exits on Church Road. Two would take him onto dual carriageways in and out of London. The other three led to local housing estates. Across the road was a train station with Overground and Underground links. But Hamish didn't head for any of them. He strolled down the footpath at the back of the buildings and stopped four houses down. He looked each way and disappeared through a gate in the wall. Digging the keys out of his pocket, he walked through the small garden to a back door. It was similar to the flat he'd just made a hasty retreat from, only this one was more lived in. And no one knew about it. Whistling, he went in and slung his bag down and walked through to the living room. Three computers had been set up on a large table. He booted them up and opened a grid of camera feeds. The top left-hand image showed a man examining the burnt-out microwave. In the bottom one, another was perched halfway up the ladder in the garden, looking up and down Church Road and talking into his headset.

'Keep looking, asshole, cause I ain't there,' Hamish whispered, as if they might hear him.

The man in the kitchen was talking on his mobile while others moved quickly around the flat.

'You look like you're in charge. Who the fuck are you, then?' Hamish said, staring at the monitor as they tore apart his flat.

He turned his attention back to the top feed and took a

screenshot of the guy on the phone, then scooted across to the third computer.

'Time to find out who you are, boss man.'

He opened the internet browser and typed in the URL for Atlantic Data Services. He logged in as Martin Thompson and the page redirected to a remote-access MI6 database.

'Thank you once again, Agent Thompson, for your security clearance.'

He was about to transfer the screenshot into the facial recognition search when a tall, dark-haired figure walked over to the mobile guy.

'Hello hello. You look familiar. What have you got me mixed up in, Snipe?'

He opened an email from Snipe with Danny Pearson's details and some kid's mobile footage of the guy taking out two policemen. He took a screenshot of Pearson and entered it along with the boss guy's details into the MI6 portal. The facial recognition search could take anything from a few minutes to several hours to produce results, so he took one last glance at the camera feeds before getting up and going to the kitchen.

'Let's give those arseholes a few hours to find nothing and fuck off, then I'll go to the pub for lunch. First, let's have a cuppa.'

He continued talking to himself—a result of too much time spent on his own, he figured, but selling secrets to the highest bidders made for a paranoid and lonely life.

CHAPTER 32

'**D**on't think much of your ready meal,' Danny said in Hamish's kitchen.

'Yes, quite. I don't think we'll find much here. He obviously knew what he was doing,' said Paul. 'Your source for this guy... do you think he tipped him off?'

'No, absolutely not.'

'Ok, sorry, had a rough night. The Prime Minister and Cabinet are going nuts over the explosions in London and the attack on our oldest bank. They want results yesterday,' said Paul.

'That's why you're paid the big bucks. Mind if I have a little look around?' Danny said, poking a finger into the burnt-out microwave.

'Knock yourself out,' Paul said, stepping out to answer his ever-ringing mobile.

Danny walked through the flat checking cupboards, draws and a wardrobe before clambering out the window to investigate Cambell's escape route. In the garden he climbed the ladder and looked over the wall. John Cummings paced around below.

'What we got out here then, John?'

'Oh, hi, Danny. Yeah, good choice of location. Plenty of exit routes and the train station. There's around six different ways to get out of here,' said John, pointing.

Danny looked around in silence. Something struck him as odd.

'Any of these parked cars arrived or left since you've been here?'

'Err, no. No one's moved. Why?'

'There's no parking spaces for forty, maybe fifty metres in either direction, right? You'd think this guy would have his car parked ready, what with the microwave and ladder all set up for a quick getaway. Right here by his drop point. He wouldn't exit on foot. That's way too dangerous. And he wouldn't use the train station—he might get stuck on a platform with nowhere to run. Plus, there's lots of CCTV,' said Danny, jumping down from the wall. As he landed, a small stab of pain reminded him that his ribs hadn't fully healed.

'You think it's staged to look like an escape point?' said John. He looked around and nodded. 'Perhaps someone was waiting for him.'

'Not enough time. He saw us coming and burned the place. No trail, and out the door seconds before we came in.'

Danny crossed the road and looked back at the brick wall and houses. 'Has Paul got his earpiece in, John?'

'Yeah, he's just been on it.'

'Get him up the ladder to the top of this wall, mate.'

Soon Paul's head appeared over the wall. 'What's up?'

'You checked this address first, right? False name, yeah?' said Danny.

'Yes, it's under Brian Dobson,' Paul said, looking puzzled.

'Rented through a letting agent?'

'Right. Where are we going with this?' Paul said impatiently.

'That flat's not lived in. It's just a base for doing business. This guy's clever,

probably ex-counter intelligence, good at making you think he's one place when he's another, that sort of thing. Get on to the agent and find out if any other properties were rented on this street around the same time as this one. It'll be under a different name but definitely at the same time.'

'On it.' Paul ducked back down the ladder.

––––––––––––

The computer had a hit on Danny Pearson. Hamish sat with his cuppa and scrolled through the information. Early army career, family, a big section of classified covering his special-ops years. Currently contracted to Greenwood Security and no current address listed.

He glanced at the camera feeds. 'Still got your heads up your arses.' He chuckled as another search result pinged. 'Ah, what have we got on you, then?'

The file had no name attached to it, just *Classified—National Security* stamped across it.

'Shit.'

Hamish printed out the file on Pearson and put it in a large envelope for later. He logged out and checked his IP address was still masked and routed through three different countries. He shut down the terminal and pulled out the power and internet connections. Later, he'd scrap the machine and build a new one, just in case of any tracers or trackers. In his game, you couldn't be too careful.

CHAPTER 33

Paul poked his head above the wall. 'Bingo. Ground-floor flat, fourth house down that way,' he said, pointing towards Danny's left. 'He rented it the same week. All correspondence was carried out over the phone and email. Deposit paid in cash and a courier collected the keys. No one actually met the client.'

Paul listened to his earpiece. 'Radio up. We're going in the front in two minutes. You two go in the back, just in case he makes a run for it. Hard and fast. I want to catch the bastard before he destroys anything.'

Paul's head ducked below the wall and he was gone again. Danny and John moved along the wall, counting the buildings until they were four houses down. Earpieces in and weapons drawn, they stood either side of the gate, waiting for Paul's countdown over the earpiece. Danny eased the latch slowly then opened it just a few millimetres and waited.

'All units, on my mark. One, two, three. Go, go, go.'

Hamish drained the last dregs of his tea and glanced across at his camera feeds. Nobody around.

'Hello. Where the fuck have you lot gone?'

The crash of the back and front doors splintering answered his question.

'Shit!'

'Armed officers. Down on your knees. Hands behind your head, now!' barked a man as a gun pointed firmly at Hamish's head.

He sank to his knees and was cuffed. They took him out the front and piled him

straight into a waiting car.

———

'Right, go through this lot with a fine-tooth comb,' said Paul. 'Danny, great job.'

Paul opened an envelope lying next to the computers and scanned the contents, then handed it to Danny.

'Come take a look,' said Paul as he picked up a driving licence with Nikali Yentski on it.

Danny thumbed through the file. It was full of information about him.

'Someone's a big fan,' said Paul, looking up and waving Tom across.

'Tom, wrap up all these PCs and take them back to HQ, please. Take Danny with you and pick up Scott Miller on the way. He's been looking at the Leamings thing for me. I'd like him to look at these too. Make them a priority.'

CHAPTER 34

Danny clicked his seat belt into place and felt a tingling sensation at the back of his neck.

'Just a sec,' he said to Tom. He scanned the road and the houses in front. Nothing. He swung round and checked behind. Still nothing. He turned back around slowly.

'What is it?' said Tom.

'I just had the feeling we're being watched. It's nothing. Let's go,' said Danny still feeling uneasy.

They drove to the end of the street and turned left at the cafe on the corner leading onto the high street.

Inside the cafe, two menus moved to one side as Snipe and Ramirez watched the Range Rover. Earlier that morning they'd stolen one of fifteen British Gas vans parked in Stratford's local depot. Their route had taken them past the unit under the arches. It had been swarming with the emergency services and scenes-of-crime officers. As they were waved through by traffic police, they'd made out the smouldering remains of the works unit and several body bags being carried to a coroner's van. Snipe had run through all possible scenarios, trying to fathom what the fuck had been going on.

'Fuck it. Let's transfer Hamish's money and pick up the new passports. The sooner we get the fuck out of the country the better,' he'd said.

Ramirez had frowned and nodded, and Snipe had opened up the bank app on his phone. Minutes had passed when a technical fault message appeared, asking all customers to contact the bank. When Snipe eventually got past the engaged tone, a recorded message had informed him that there'd been a cyberattack on the bank, that statements would speed up his account recovery and that he should expect long delays. A stream of profanities had exploded before he'd smashed his phone on the van's dash. Reality had quickly sunk in. Marcus had screwed them. Snipe had punched the dash until the plastic cracked, while Ramirez called Hamish to tell him they were on their way with cash for the passports and ID. Hamish had let slip that Marcus was going to America and asked if they were going with him. Ramirez immediately offered more cash for information and Hamish had agreed to ping them a copy of Marcus's American passport. Despite having the cash to pay Hamish stashed in various safety-deposit boxes dotted around London, they'd had every intention of collecting the passports and slitting Hamish's throat. Half an hour later, they'd turned the British Gas van onto the Hamish's road... just in time to see him being marched out in handcuffs and shoved into a blacked-out Range Rover by armed officers. Ramirez had driven calmly past and parked around the corner on the high street. They'd taken a seat in the cafe on the corner and ordered bacon rolls and mugs of tea. The window gave them the perfect view of the MI6 unit going in and out of two flats. Then Danny Pearson had exited one of the flats and got into a Range Rover with another man. From behind his menu, Snipe was ready to explode.

'I swear I'm going to kill that motherfucker,' he said, fighting to calm himself. The muscles in his face eventually relaxed. 'But first, we go to America. We'll have to risk the passports we used for Japan. We're going to get our money back and kill that smug bastard Marcus slowly and painfully.'

With a deep sigh, he sat back and ate his bacon roll.

CHAPTER 35

B ack at HQ, people combed through Cambell's
property, cataloguing the items according to the
level of importance. Scott was thrilled with the
prospect of cracking the bad guys' computers and settled
down to show off his superior IT skills to the unit's resident
whizz kids, Glen Silverman and Trevor Ackley. He breezed
through the encryption and passwords. The files unlocked
a wealth of information: pictures and identities, including
Tenby's new one; a list of all the passports, IDs, equipment
and explosives purchased by Peters and his team; and the
dates and details of each transaction. Upstairs in a
makeshift interview room, Edward and Paul bombarded
Cambell with the evidence against him. With the game up,
he resigned himself to a deal. In exchange for witness
protection and a new identity, he'd give them enough information to put more than a dozen high-profile criminals
away, and tell them all he knew about Tenby's American
contact. Edward headed off for meetings with the powers-
that-be who could authorise such a deal; only when the

deal was assured would Hamish start talking. Meanwhile, a forensic report identified the body in the transit as one David Peters. Ex-special forces—dishonourably discharged. To add to the list of surprises, Tom pulled reports from Scotland Yard's serious-crime unit about the burnt-out unit in Stratford. They had discovered five bodies. Two had been identified as Kadah and Barzan Naser.

At 5 o'clock Paul arrived back at HQ after a long meeting with the Prime Minister and members of the security council. The threat of an international financial cyberattack had rippled through to the top brass on both sides of the Atlantic.

'Gather round, everybody, please,' said Edward, raising his voice above the buzz of the room. 'Okay, pipe down, people. This is the state of play. US Immigration has confirmed that Marcus Tenby entered the USA this morning via JFK under the new identity of Terence Blake.' Edward pointed to a blown-up image of the passport picture. 'I think it's safe to assume that Tenby has cleaned house, killing everyone associated with him, and is now working to his own agenda. He has at least one American contact, a hacker known as Spider. Nicholas Snipe and Paulo Ramirez's whereabouts are still unknown. According to Cambell, they were coming to pick up new passports and IDs at the time of our raid. It's believed they may have been double-crossed by Tenby and are en route to New York in pursuit of him.'

Edward turned and nodded to Paul, who opened a folder and took centre stage.

'Right, Edward and I, plus a unit of four, are off to

New York to assist the FBI in a joint Anglo-American operation. Our contact is FBI Agent Patrick Fallen, he's been
tasked with finding Tenby. The four of you accompanying
us will be Danny, Tom, John, and Glen. The flight is
booked for 8.00 a.m. from Heathrow. Simon and Trevor, if
you could pick us up in the two Range Rovers in the morning, please. The rest of you are to follow any leads and
liaise with us Stateside. Scott, your continued assistance
with T.A. Leamings and their systems provider, MSI Software, would be most appreciated. They've already agreed
to cover all your costs.'

———

The taxi was heading for Scott's place first, then it would
be on to Rob's.

Danny, uncharacteristically quiet on the journey, finally
spoke.

'I've got a favour to ask you.'

Scott turned to face him, intrigued.

'When you're at Leamings, I need you to find and
restore an offshore account for me. It's for someone who
can't declare it. You have to trust me—he's a good guy and
we owe him.'

'Whatever you need,' said Scott. 'It's only a matter of
time before I crack the virus code and gain access. I
wouldn't be here if it wasn't for you, old chap. Give me the
details and leave it with me.'

Danny smiled at his friend. 'Cheers, buddy. I think
Tenby chose Leamings for a reason, maybe to cover his
tracks, payments in or out. You know what they say—
follow the money and find the man.'

Scott looked deep in thought for a moment.

'Yes, jolly good thinking. I'll get straight on it tomorrow. I'll call if I find anything.' Danny helped him out of the taxi and watched him limp on his crutches into his apartment building before he told the taxi driver to move off.

CHAPTER 36

The eight-hour British Airways flight from Heathrow to JFK was uneventful. The six- strong team looked a little out of place among the transatlantic executives and wealthy pensioner tourists in business class, and their banter received some disapproving mumbles and glances from the suits opposite. Danny and Tom threw them a withering look, and the suits kept their eyes facing firmly forward for the rest of the flight. In the arrivals terminal, at the end of the line of taxi drivers, chauffeurs and expectant business associates with name cards in hand, stood a tall, sandy-haired man in a trade-mark black suit, white shirt and black tie. The name *Edward Jenkins* was written neatly on the sign in front of him. Leading the team, Edward walked briskly towards him, his hand outstretched.

'Edward Jenkins. Pleasure to meet you.'

'Patrick Fallen. Good to meet you too. If you gentlemen would like to follow me, we have transport waiting for you.'

Two more black-suited men stepped forward to escort

them to a couple of awaiting Chrysler SUVs. Fallen laid out the plan for the day. He'd take them to the FBI building and introduce them to the team tasked with locating Tenby. After the briefing, he'd drive them to the Hilton. Danny enjoyed the sights as they drove. He'd never been to New York and the view of the skyline as they crossed Brooklyn Bridge took his breath away. They pulled up at the impressive forty-one storey building on Federal Plaza. In the foyer, they went through the obligatory pat-downs and metal detectors before being escorted to a large task room on the thirty-sixth floor. Twenty agents milled about in different directions, engrossed in their individual tasks. The room was laden with terminals and large inter-active monitors—a cut above London's low-key white-boards and pin boards—that offered a hi-tech information flow that could be opened, pinched, zoomed and amended with just the touch of a screen. Danny scanned the pictures. His gaze landed on an image of Marcus Tenby now Terence Blake. A right-pointing arrow drew him to the familiar faces of Kadah and Barzan Naser. They'd written the word *Dead* below the pictures. A line connected them and Tenby to a picture of Akbar Bakr, leader of The Faith, *Killed in suicide-bomb attack* written beneath. Above that was another image, this time of Shan Al Amat with *suicide bomber* written below it. Danny stared at the connec-tions, thinking, then followed a line from Tenby to the left. It led to a blank square. The note above read: *Spider?* They'd lined up five photographs below it, each with an identity beside it. Fallen did the introductions and so began an hour-long exchange of information, including what was known about Spider. The renowned hacker was believed to be responsible for various hacks into large organisations such as New York's traffic management system, the subway, even the computer managing the elevator in the Empire

State Building. A terrified tourist had been trapped on a continuous up and down trip for an hour before they could shut the lift down. Spider's identity was still unknown, but they had selected five suspects based on analyses of social media content, school and university files, and police reports and convictions. Fallen had been given huge resources: the FBI, Homeland Security and the NYPD. Hundreds of Tenby's old and new IDs had been distributed. Everyone was looking for him. Danny wondered whether his and the team's invitation to New York was more of a political token rather than a necessary contribution to the investigation. With the debrief done and jet lag setting in, someone drove them to the hotel for some rest.

CHAPTER 37

Danny's room was modern and spacious and had a stunning view of Central Park. It had just gone 6.00 p.m. and the sun was setting, casting an orange glow across the skyscrapers and park. It was eleven back home, so he pulled his phone out and texted Trisha: *Wonderful view from the hotel. Only thing missing is you.* He'd just pressed send when another message pinged in from Scott: *Favour done. Followed the rabbit down the hole and found the Mad Hatter. Call me. Need to talk.* As tired as he was, the cryptic text made him chuckle. He punched in the number and Scott answered immediately.

'I take it you found something out about Tenby then,' Danny said.

'Is it safe to talk, old boy?'

'Yes, perfectly safe. I'm not a spy in a Cold War thriller,' said Danny, walking over to the window to watch the sun set over the city.

'Err, okay, I suppose not.' Scott sounded slightly disappointed.

'What you got for me, Scotty boy?'

'Right, yes, well I recruited help from some banking colleagues. After the Leamings attack, they were happy to help on an off-the-record basis. We started with CMS, going back to just before former owner Chris Mayhew's wife and children died. With a lot of digging we found several large payments through a series of dummy companies that eventually led back to Syria. I then looked at payments from CMS to Tenby and Kadah, and payments they made from their accounts. And I found a small slip-up: a payment to and a money transfer from a company that, surprise surprise, turned out to be another dummy account. That account had large fund transfers leading back to—guess where—Syria. I believe that was Tenby's funding account. There are payments to Hamish Cambell and to an offshore account belonging to the brutes who tried to kill me. But this is the interesting bit... when Tenby hit Leamings, he created an access hole that emptied one point eight million from that account.' Scott paused for a moment.

'Wow, that'll piss Snipe off. He'll come for Tenby for sure,' said Danny.

'That's not all. I continued to follow the money and found a string of large payments, starting six months ago, to a New York IT company named Deckland Consultants. They opened the account and the company at the same time at the New York Commercial Bank. I have the branch code and address. Coincidently, Tenby bought tickets to New York from the CMS account two days prior to that,' said Scott.

Danny whistled. 'Scott, you're worth every penny they pay you, mate. Definitely the dog's bollocks.'

'There's a cherry on top,' said Scott. 'Deckland has been making payments to one Andrew Pitt and one Shane

Wallace. I'm guessing they're the American accomplices preparing the main terrorist attack.'

Danny thought for a minute.

'I don't think it's terrorism, mate. I think it's been about revenge all along. He's taken revenge on everyone who's wronged him throughout his life. America is last on his list, for killing his parents. He's going to cripple the country while robbing it of God knows how much before disappearing forever,' said Danny watching out the window as the world grew dark outside. 'The pub lunch is on me when I get back, mate. Can you email me all that when you get a minute?'

'Already on its way, old man,' Scott laughed. 'And I want starters and a dessert.' 'You got it, buddy. Gotta go.'

Danny hung up as Scott's email pinged onto the screen.

He showered and changed, then spotted the message from Trisha: *Love you*. He smiled, texted the endearment back, and headed down for dinner with Paul and the team. Beer in hand, he filled them in on Scott's revelations. Paul and Edward agreed to pass on the information to Fallen in the morning. When everyone was fed and watered, they dispersed to their rooms. Danny climbed into bed and sent one last text: *Hi, Harry. Check a certain savings account. Thanks for your help. Your favourite nephew.*

CHAPTER 38

n a side alley in Jamaica, Queens, the sound of grunts and groans broke the early morning quiet. Three members of the Lucre Mafia family lay on the ground. One, a short stocky man, was curled foetal-like in agony, unable to move his broken arm. The other clutched the leaking stab wound in his chest. He gurgled as he writhed, unable to draw air into his blood-filled lungs. A taller man lay motionless. A bullet had ripped through one eye and a mess of brain tissue dripped down the wall behind him. Ramirez was calmly choking out a fourth man. Snipe pushed a gun against the forehead of the guy with the broken arm.

'Where do I find this hacker, Spider?' he said.

A trickle of urine stained the terrified man's trouser leg and flowed down the alley.

'You dirty bastard, fucking tell me where Spider is or I'll pull the trigger,' said Snipe, growling as he pushed the gun harder into his head.

'Okay, okay. We used to meet him at an internet cafe, Cyber Time, on Bay Parkway down in Brooklyn. He said it was his local. That's all I know. Please let me go. I ain't seen nothing here. Please,' he said feebly as tears rolled down his cheeks.

This only infuriated Snipe further.

'Stop whining and die like a man, you gutless wanker.' His piquing temper caused his gun hand to shake.

The words seemed to take a second to sink in, then his eyes widened, and his mouth opened. Snipe pulled the trigger.

'Let's go, Rami,' he said, as if nothing had happened.

Ramirez twisted the semi-conscious man's neck. There was a sickening crack and he let him slide to the floor. He picked up the man's gun and tucked it in his jacket.

Without looking back, the two men walked casually out of the alley.

CHAPTER 39

After a good night's sleep in the luxury king-sized bed, Danny's aches and pains had reduced to a niggle. Feeling refreshed, he joined the others in the breakfast hall for a full English breakfast. The discussion turned to what Danny had learned from Scott.

'What do you reckon, Paul?' said Tom.

'I think we should get a warrant to access the accounts of Andrew Pitt and Shane Wallace and follow any transactions or card payments. That will help us narrow in on their location,' said Paul.

'Fallen will do the same through Homeland Security. The big question is, how involved is he going to let us get?' Danny said.

That dampened the mood around the table. After a brief pause, Edward spoke. 'How about Paul, John and myself keep Fallen busy with Scott's information? In the meantime, you, Tom, and Glen take a little trip to the New York Commercial Bank and check out the area. Poke around. Maybe it's close to where he's staying or close to this Spider character.'

Paul nodded. 'We'll stay in the command centre and phone you with any updates.'

————

At 10.00 a.m. Danny, Tom, and Glen spilled out of the yellow cab at 8622 Bay Parkway, Brooklyn. In front of them stood the branch of the New York Commercial Bank that Tenby had visited. Danny paid the taxi driver and couldn't help but smile when the driver shouted, 'Have a nice day!'

The bank was small and unimposing. It was located at the end of the high street, between shops and a row of residential buildings that stretched all the way down to the bay. Further up Bay Parkway, under the train line that ran over the top of Eighty- Sixth Street, they could see a Citibank on one side and a TD Bank on the other side. More shops and businesses stretched up into a bustling high street.

'I think that's a Chase Bank further up there,' said Glen.

'A lot of banks. I wonder what's special about this one,' said Danny.

'Maybe nothing. Could just be the first one he came to.'

'Could be. It's a bit off the beaten track. This is all we have so let's assume he's setting up a base near here or he met Spider around here. Or both.'

'Okay, if he's in this area, what equipment would he need to launch his attack and what kind of base would he need to use it?' said Tom.

'That's a very good question,' said Danny, pulling out his phone. He spied a security guard through the bank's sliding doors.

'Hey, Tom, do us a favour, have a chat with that security guard. See if he recognises Tenby from any of the images.'

Tom went off with Glen into the bank while Danny rang Paul.

'Hi, Trisha. Everything okay at the office? Wait a minute. I'll just go somewhere quiet,' answered Paul, followed by a muffled silence. 'Hey, Danny. Been a tense morning. Our American friends got very excited about the information we gave them. However, their noses are out of joint a tad because it was us that found it. And Fallen wasn't happy about half his visiting party going sightseeing. Anyway, what's up?'

'It's too early in the UK to call Scott, so I need one of you there to go through the account data. See if there's been any large computer equipment orders placed online or locally, and sent here starting around six months ago,' said Danny.

'Okay. You on to something?' said Paul.

'Maybe. The bank's an odd choice, not on any main bus or train routes. How did he even find it? Unless he's local, or his base is. He needs a lot of computer gear to launch this attack. I'm hoping three and a half thousand miles from London, Tenby thought he was safe, and either bought equipment here or online. If we're really lucky, he may have had it delivered.'

'On it. I'll call you in a bit.'

Tom came back out of the bank, smiling.

'Anything?' Danny said.

'Nothing on the old Tenby photo but the Terence Blake ID came up trumps. He was in there two days ago with a young man in his twenties—long dark hair, grungy, black t-shirt, ripped jeans, black boots. The security guard remembered them clearly because the young guy was arguing with Tenby before they withdrew a large amount of cash,' said Tom.

'Right, let's carry on with the assumption that they're local. I say we split up and show Tenby's photo to property-letting agents; ask about short-term commercial lets. And computer stores too. See if they bought any equipment.'

'Sounds good to me,' said Glen, and Tom nodded.

They split up. Danny headed across the intersection under the train tracks and up Bay Parkway, while Tom and Glen took Eighty-Sixth Street.

CHAPTER 40

Snipe walked into Cyber Time, casting an imposing silhouette in the doorway as the sunlight beat down behind him. Some of the customers turned to look. Ramirez had positioned himself across the street on a bench about twenty metres away. He had a good view up and down Bay Parkway, and the junction with Eighty-Sixth Street was only eighty metres away. Snipe wore jeans, an *I Love New York* t- shirt, and a Nike baseball cap. A ruck-sack was slung over one shoulder. Fifteen computer booths lined the room in an L-shape. It was a quiet morning and only three were occupied. The centre space was filled with brightly painted old kitchen tables and mismatched wooden chairs. Only one was occupied; a bunch of scruffy students shared sodas and flicked through study books. They stared and sniggered. Snipe stared back, plunging them into a nervous silence. Satisfied he'd put the fear of God into them, he walked to the counter and put his ruck-sack on top. A bearded hippy who looked to be in his fifties greeted him.

'Hi, I'm Mel. Can I help you?'

'Yes, mate. I'm looking for a young guy who hangs out here: early twenties, grungy, long dark hair, a tattoo of a spider sitting on a computer mouse on his right wrist. Calls himself Spider sometimes.'

'Yeah, he comes in here every so often. What do you want him for?' said Mel cautiously.

'I've got a job for him,' said Snipe. He spotted a sign on the back wall—*Open an account and get 60 minutes free*—and pointed at it. 'What do you need for me to get that?'

'Oh, just a photo ID and something with your address on it, like a bill or bank statement. You wanna open one?' said Mel, turning to his PC.

Snipe put his hand inside the rucksack, but instead of ID he pulled out a gun.

'Don't panic, matey boy. Just pull up Spider's real name and address, and a copy of his photo ID, and I'll be on my merry way.'

His arm shot out sideways, gun pointing steady as a rock. One of the students had his phone raised.

'Touch that record button, sonny, and I'm gonna play *Call of Duty* with you for real. And I never lose,' Snipe growled, his eyes never leaving Mel's.

The students dropped their phones like they were on fire and froze.

CHAPTER 41

aving had no success with his third letting agent, Danny took in the shops and businesses further up the street and wondered how his teammates were getting on. He glanced back in the direction he'd come from. And saw Ramirez. He was sitting on a bench fifty metres down the street. Danny's spine tingled. Ramirez got up as Snipe emerged from a cyber cafe opposite. They got into the front of a yellow cab, Snipe behind the wheel, and drove away, turning left onto Eighty- Sixth Street before disappearing around the corner. A group of youths exited the cafe and ran crying down the street in a panic. Danny hurried towards the cafe, dialling Paul as he moved.

'Get Fallen and the team to a cafe on Bay Parkway. Cyber Time. Snipe and Ramirez just left in a big hurry.'

Danny hung up and burst through the doorway. A group of students jumped out of their skins. He flashed his FBI visitor pass. 'FBI! It's okay. Police and agents are on their way.' The flash of ID seemed to pacify them, and he went to the counter and peered over. A man sat on the floor, holding his head. Blood seeped through his fingers and down his cheek. Danny grabbed a bunch of serviettes and moved behind the counter. He squatted and moved the guy's hand and pressed the serviettes onto the gash in his head.

'Keep the pressure on it. What's your name, mate?' he said, placing the man's hand back over the makeshift dressing.

'Mel.'

'What did he want, Mel—the big guy?' Danny said.

Mel looked up and pointed at the computer. 'The name and address of a customer. I gave it to him and he still side-swiped me with his gun. Bastard.' Danny looked at the screen with Andrew Pitt's profile spread across it. 'Does he sometimes call himself Spider?' Danny said.

Mel winced. 'Yeah, that's him. I knew he was trouble.'

Danny stood up and took a photo of the screen before calling Paul. Tom and Glen burst through the door, as Paul answered.

'We're less than ten minutes away,' said Paul over sirens and engine noise.

'We haven't got ten minutes. Snipe's got Spider's name, address, and photo. I think they're going for him now.'

'Danny, this is Fallen. Was Spider's real name on our list?'

Danny thought back to the command centre. 'Yes, it's Andrew Pitt,' he said.

'Good—we've had all the names under surveillance. There's a team already there. I'm sending extra agents now. Stay there, we'll be with you in a couple of minutes.'

Fallen hung up.

CHAPTER 42

Snipe and Ramirez pulled their stolen taxi over to the kerb on Twenty-First Drive. Within seconds, they'd clocked the two FBI agents parked a short distance ahead in a black Chrysler.

'Shock and awe, Rami. Quick in and out,' Snipe said, pulling a large serrated commando knife from his bag with one hand and tucking his gun in the back of his jeans with the other.

Ramirez followed his lead, pulling a similar knife from his jacket before checking his gun in its shoulder holster. They nodded at each other.

'We've got about five minutes before the shit hits the fan,' said Snipe, climbing out of the taxi.

Ramirez got out the other side. Knives in hand and stooping low, they ran full pelt towards the rear of the Chrysler, covering the distance in seconds. Snipe swung to the left side, Ramirez to the right. In unison, they struck the two windows with the butts of their knives. The glassed exploded in a shower of crystals. The two agents inside froze, the one in the passenger seat still on the phone as

Snipe and Ramirez ferociously pummelled their commando knives into their necks and chest. Within seconds they were on the move again, flat out to the door to the apartments. Ramirez stabbed at the buzzers until one was answered.

'Yep,' said a tinny voice.

'UPS parcel for you, sir,' said Snipe.

The lock buzzed open. Twenty seconds after exiting the stolen taxi, the two stormed in and bounded up the stairs, two at a time. The door to 226 opened and a small Italian-looking man stepped out.

'You gotta parcel for me?'

In one smooth movement, Snipe stabbed his commando knife through the side of the man's throat and sliced it forwards, severing the windpipe and arteries, rendering the man unable to make a sound as he bled to death. By the time he hit the ground, they were up to 238. Snipe shouldered the door. The wood splintered and the door burst open. Guns levelled, they swept the apartment. Rooted to the sofa was a trembling, skinny blonde with spiked hair, dark eye-makeup and multiple piercings.

'Who are you?' said Snipe, placing the barrel of his gun inches away from her face. 'WHO THE FUCK ARE YOU?'

'Lisa,' she said feebly.

'Who are you to Andrew Pitt?' Snipe growled.

'I'm his girlfriend.'

Snipe leaned in and stared at her.

'Do you know where he is?'

'N-no, I don't.'

Snipe fumed. 'Do you know how to get in contact with him?'

'Yes,' she said.

Snipe's blow knocked her clean out like a rag doll. He

grabbed the phone lying on the sofa and threw the girl over his shoulder.

'Exit. Rami, you take point.'

Another twenty seconds and they were down the stairs and out. As the sound of the sirens grew closer, Ramirez pulled the taxi out of the estate and into the endless flow of yellow cabs on the main road making their way to the city centre. Hidden in plain sight.

CHAPTER 43

At the end of Bay Forty-First Street, Brooklyn, sat a closed-down auto-repair shop. The building looked dull, abandoned. Its four corrugated shutters were thick with rust and the windows of the reception area had been painted over. In the small boating marina to the rear, gleaming white yachts and multi-coloured speed boats were moored. The building had been empty for three years so when Marcus had called out of the blue, offering a cash deposit and three months' rent upfront, the letting agents had hurriedly agreed. The bays that had once housed car ramps and mechanics now contained eight six-foot-high server cabinets, each with its own super-fast fibre internet feed. In front of each cabinet, lined up on a row of fold-up tables, were ten of the most powerful Dell computers money could buy. Cables snaked between the computers and cabinets. Marcus was finishing work on the feeds from the last of the eighty computers needed to launch his attack on America's banks—a final act of revenge that would net him $500 billion and leave their systems crippled beyond repair.

Not a one-man job. Spider and university friend, Shane Wallace, ran checks on the Dells while he fiddled with the server cabinet.

Spider was on his phone again. His lack of discipline and argumentative attitude infuriated Marcus. If he hadn't been a truly gifted hacker he'd have been dead by now. Still, he wished he didn't need Spider for his plan. Shane was easier to deal with, and clever, though not in the same league as Spider.

'Spider get off the phone and run a protocol check,' shouted Marcus.

He got no response.

'Andrew, get off the phone. Now!' Calling him Andrew would annoy him.

'In a minute, Marcus. I'm checking something out,' said Spider, without lifting his head from his phone.

'Don't call me Marcus, you little shit. It's Terence Blake now. Only Terence.'

'Yeah, well, don't call me Andrew, you old... Shit, shit. Marcus—I mean Terence—come here quick. My mate's just sent me some photos of this massive fucker. He tore up Cyber Time at gunpoint. He was looking for me.'

The colour drained from Spider's face. Marcus grabbed the phone and viewed the shaky pictures of Snipe questioning the cafe owner and striking him with the butt of his gun.

'What would he have got?' said Marcus, handing the phone to Shane who was dying to look.

'Err, I don't know. Shit, they have my address. And Lisa's at home. Gimme the phone! I've gotta call her and tell her to get out. Shane, give me the fucking phone!' said Spider, grabbing it off him and tapping the call button as he paced around nervously.

160

'Spider, me old mucker. You're a hard man to find. Now just listen and do what you're told or I'm going to have some fun with Lisa here. If Marcus is there, just say *Where are you?* and then say *Okay. Go to your mum's. I'll call you in a bit,*' said Snipe.

'Where are you? Okay. Go to your mum's and stay there. I'll call you in a bit,' said Spider.

'Good boy. Don't do anything stupid. It's Marcus I want but I'll gut your girlfriend if I have to. Hang up and call me in an hour with no one around.' The call ended.

'Is everything okay, Spider?' Marcus sounded suspicious.

'Yeah, she was round her mate's. I'll give her a call in an hour. Who the fuck is that guy? Do you recognise him?' he said, sucking it up and trying to sound as convincing as possible.

'No, I've never seen him before,' Marcus said.

'Okay if I stay at yours, Shane? I wanna give my place some distance.' Shane nodded. Marcus turned back to the server rack.

An hour later, Spider had offered to do the coffee run. Now he shuffled along the footbridge over the busy Belt Parkway dual carriageway. When the traffic noise had died down and he was on Twenty-Seventh Avenue, he called Lisa's mobile.

'Where's Lisa? You better not have hurt her, you bastard.'

'Whoa, slow down there, Cockroach or Bug or whatever the fuck your nickname is. Keep your mouth shut and

161

ears open and do what I say, or you'll be finding bits of your girlfriend all over Brooklyn,' said Snipe, grinning at the petrified girl tied and gagged on the bed.

Ramirez was in the kitchenette on one side of the lounge area. He was cleaning and sharpening the commando knives they'd used in the assault on Spider's apartment.

'Okay, okay. Just don't hurt her,' Spider pleaded.

'Right, shut up. This is how it's gonna go. I ask you a question and you answer it. No bullshit because I can smell bullshit a mile off. When is Marcus planning his attack?'

'I-I-I don't know—'

'Yep, I smell bullshit. For that I'll cut your girlfriend's ear off.'

He got up, leaned over her, and pinched one of the rings in her ear tightly. It ripped through the fleshy lobe and Lisa screamed through her gag. Snipe held the phone in front of her so Spider could hear.

'No, wait! It's the day after tomorrow. Don't hurt her. It's midday, the day after tomorrow.'

The kid sounded desperate. Snipe could imagine the sense of helplessness that washed over him, and smirked.

'Next question. What's the address for the server base?'

Snipe gave Lisa a small kidney punch, and she let out a muffled squeal.

'Don't! It's the old Bay Motors building on Bay Forty-First Street... by the kids' funfair. Please don't hurt her!'

'Listen, Cockroach, this is what you're going to do: you're going to carry on like nothing's happened and you're going to text this number an hour before the attack. When it all kicks off, we'll take care of Marcus and you're going to put a considerable sum of money in our account. You following this?'

'Yes, I follow you,' came Spider's feeble reply.

'Good. For that, you'll get your girlfriend back, a cut of the money, and the freedom to go your merry way. Okay?'

Snipe waited just long enough to hear Spider's confirmation, then hung up.

'All set, Rami. Day after tomorrow and it's done.'

'Good. We need to ditch the Toyota and buy a car for the drive down to Mexico once it's over.'

'Yeah, okay. I'm gonna do a reconnaissance of the server site later for final planning.'

He leered at Lisa, then brought his mouth close to her ear. 'You and me are going to have some fun later,' he whispered as he squeezed her breast. The fear in her eyes fuelled the excitement in his twisted mind.

CHAPTER 44

anny and the team had regrouped outside
Spider's apartment. Groups of FBI and NYPD
officers filled the area around them. Tensions
were running high. Two agents had been brutally
murdered, and a member of the public's throat had been
torn out.

Fallen came over to Danny, his face ashen. He looked
like he'd aged ten years. 'What kind of animal does this?'
he said.

'Special forces. A trained psychopath. Shock and awe.
It's an all-out attack. Time's short. You go in with
maximum speed and power, wipe out anything that stands
in your way, and leave. I doubt they were here more than a
few minutes,' said Danny matter-of-factly. The expression
on Fallen's face revealed a new understanding of Danny's
talents.

'Was anyone at home?' said Danny, ignoring the
awkward silence. He was unashamed of his past services to
his country.

'Pitt left early this morning—gave one of our agents

the slip through the alleyways behind the apartments. Doyle and Trent reported in just before they were murdered—they said Pitt's girlfriend, Lisa O'Hanlin, was still in the apartment. That was at nine-thirty this morning, so we're not sure if she was still there when Snipe and Ramirez got here,' said Fallen, waving in the black crime-scene van that had come to collect the bodies.

'Can we have a look around the apartment?' said Danny.

Fallen thought for a moment. 'Just you and Paul and touch nothing. I don't want you contaminating the crime scene.'

Fallen showed them into the building and shouted up to the agents on the door to let them in. They climbed the stairs, edging around the large pool of drying blood on the second-floor landing, and continuing up to Spider's apartment. The door was hanging loosely off its hinges, but there were no signs that the interior had been turned over. This suggested that Snipe had entered, found Lisa O'Hanlin and taken her. If the place had been empty, they'd have torn it apart, looking for anything to help them find Spider. There was a small table beside the sofa in the living room. On it stood a half-full cup of coffee with a lipstick smudge around the rim. Beside it was a crisp new ladies Fitbit box, open and empty. Tucked underneath was a piece of notepaper with a partial email address and number. Danny looked around to check that no one was looking, then slipped the scrap into his pocket. He found Paul, and they went back downstairs. After thanking Fallen, the team headed towards the main road.

Paul turned to Danny. 'Well?'

Danny gave him a sideways grin. 'Never could get anything past you.' He pulled the piece of paper out of his pocket. 'I'm fairly sure Lisa O'Hanlin is wearing a Fitbit.

I'm hoping the scribbles on this contain the details to the Fitbit account.'

The team looked blankly at him.

'Okay, so the Fitbit has sensors and GPS built in, which downloads your data to the app when your phone's on. Sign into the Fitbit account on a PC and it'll show you your exercise data and where you were when you did it.'

'What do we do with it? My laptop's back at the hotel,' Glen said.

'Not enough time. If Snipe's got Lisa, time's short. I need to get Scott on it,' said Danny.

He took a photo of the note and pinged it to Scott with a message: *Need this Fitbit account cracked and any GPS data on location ASAP. Life and death. Call me when you have something.*

His phoned buzzed seconds later: *On it now. Password's going to take a while to crack. Call you soon.*

'Let's go back to the hotel and get something to eat while we wait,' said Edward, waving down some taxis.

———

The rest of the team had already retired for the night. Only Danny and Tom remained in the bar. They'd hit it off straightaway, Danny being ex-SAS and Tom an ex-corporal in the paras. The stories of combat flowed with an easy understanding. An incoming call interrupted their merriment.

'Hi, mate. What've you got for me?' said Danny.

'I cracked Lisa O'Hanlin's Fitbit account, old boy,' said Scott.

'I never doubted you would. Now put me out of my misery and tell me if you got any GPS logs.'

'No, I'm afraid not... not off the fitness app,' said Scott.

'Shit. Well thanks for trying, Scott,' said Danny, sitting back deflated.

'No, old man. That's not all. I hacked her account and found her mobile number. I called your UK colleagues and got Trevor Ackley on it. We've been onto Vodafone. Since her abduction, the phone's been turned on three times. The last two occurred at the same location. I'm sending you the co-ordinates now. Trevor's requested the call registry and should have it in the next couple of hours.' Scott sounded nothing short of triumphant.

'Outstanding, mate. I could bloody kiss you,' said Danny.

'I'll pass on the kiss. You can owe me yet another lunch.'

'You're on.'

Danny took a big swig of beer, then relayed the information to Tom. They stared at the co-ordinates.

'Should we wake Edward or Paul?' said Tom.

'We could, or we could do a reccy ourselves. Check it out,' said Danny, a grin creeping across his face.

Tom returned the smile and stood up. 'Let's get us a cab.'

CHAPTER 45

Twenty minutes later they climbed out of a yellow cab on a quiet suburban street five minutes' walk from the location Scott had sent. They used the walking time as they would in combat—to allow their eyes to adjust to the darkness, improving their natural night vision.Danny enlarged the map as far as it would go on his phone screen. The GPS narrowed down the location to one of three four-floor apartment blocks. Each had a locked communal entrance door next to a shiny stainless-steel intercom panel.

'What now?' said Tom.

'Hmm, twelve apartments. If we assume they rented one, I can check the intercoms and look for the ones with no names on, narrow it down a bit,' said Danny.

Tom nodded.

Danny moved a fraction out of the shadows then pulled back sharply into the dark as the middle block opened. Snipe bounced down the steps and swaggered across the street. He turned and nodded to a shadowy figure in the window of the first-floor apartment, then got into a beaten-up blue Toyota and drove off. The figure in the window stared down at the street for a minute before disappearing behind the curtains.

'Shit. Better call it in. Paul or Edward can get Fallen out of bed. Let him send the heavy squad in,' said Tom.

Danny didn't move.

'You stay here and call it in. I'm going in for a closer look. Spider's girlfriend's in trouble in there,' said Danny.

He headed towards the apartment entrance.

'Danny, don't. Wait for backup,' Tom said in a loud whisper.

'Just call it in and sit tight. Anyone other than me comes out, twat 'em.'

He hugged the front of the building so he wouldn't be seen from the apartment window, then climbed the steps to the front door. Pulling out his phone he turned on the light. The door had a standard buzz lock and latch, but it was old and the frame was a little loose. Danny put his back against the brick porch surrounding the door. Pressing with one foot firmly on the centre of the door and the other just above it. Sucking up three big breaths, he braced himself, forcing the pressure through his legs and against the door. The frame flexed just enough and the lock popped. He dropped to his feet, shuffled forwards and stopped at the bottom of the stairs, listening to the building. Other than the distant murmur of a TV, all was quiet. He moved silently up the stairs to the first-floor apartment. Light spilled from the crack between the floor and the door. He watched for a minute or so but saw no crossing shadows to suggest that anyone was moving close by on the other side. He weighed up his options. They boiled down to two. Either wait for re- enforcements or attack. Memories of what Snipe liked to do to women made the decision for him. He backed up and charged. The momentum twisted the frame. The wood split and the door exploded inwards. Danny eyed his target, sped into the lounge and launched himself over the sofa at Ramirez. They collided hard. A leg snapped off the table and a chair disintegrated as Ramirez crashed through them, Danny on top of him. A commando knife flew into the air and struck the breakfast bar. Another rattled across the floor. Danny threw a fast combination of punches to Ramirez's sides and head that would have put any normal man down. Not Ramirez. He blocked the head shot with his forearm and countered with two lightning jabs to Danny's ribs, knocking him off balance. He whipped forward, head-butting Danny on the bridge of his nose. Danny fell backwards onto his arse. Ramirez flipped upright grabbing the commando knife from the breakfast bar, his face murderous. Danny shook his head to right his vision. Ramirez was coming towards him, the razor-sharp knife in hand. Danny scooped up the broken chair leg and brandished it like a police baton, flicked it up to block the knife, then countered with a kidney jab. Ramirez grunted, moved backwards, and lunged low. Danny blocked, giving Ramirez an opening. A vicious punch found his temple, sending him reeling onto the sofa. As he fell, he spotted the other commando knife and dived over the sofa to grab it. Danny stood slowly and fixed his gaze on Ramirez, who was picking up the other broken chair leg. Ramirez stared straight back. Hard as granite. Both armed with a knife and baton, they went at each other with a volley of blistering attacks and blocks. Seconds later they split, stood back, and stared at each other. Ramirez broke first, swinging the chair leg then lunging with the knife. Danny's arm blocked the attack, exposing his middle. Ramirez kicked him with the heel of his boot. Danny careened backwards through the bedroom door, his knife clattering across the floor. He fell on his back next to the bound girl on the bed. She looked him, eyes wide with terror. Ramirez dropped his chair leg and jumped on Danny, clasping the hilt of the knife with both hands, driving it towards Danny's heart. Danny caught both his wrists as the blade came close. He locked his elbows as Ramirez pushed and brought his knee up hard into Ramirez's groin, then swung him to one side. The knife plunged deep into the mattress inches from Lisa's face. Ramirez toppled onto Lisa and Danny punched him in the throat. He grabbed Ramirez's arm and pushed it up with all his might until the shoulder popped out of the socket. Ramirez's screams were cut short as Danny rained down blow after blow to his head. Ramirez's eyes rolled back in his head. Beyond rational thought, Danny pulled the knife from the mattress, ready to plunge it through Ramirez's eye and into his brain.

'Danny, don't!'

It was Tom. Multiple voices shouted, 'Armed police! Drop your weapon, now!'

A few seconds later, the tension left Danny's body, and the rage died. He threw the knife to the floor and stepped away from the bed. The cops were about to jump him and cuff him when Fallen burst in.

'Not him. He's with us.'

CHAPTER 46

The NYPD police car pulled up outside the apartment at 2.00 a.m. The officer wound down the window.

'Hey, Dev, you up there?'

The entrance door opened, and Devon Michaels plodded down the steps.

'Hiya, Ray. You got my coffee?'

'Yeah. One for Mitch as well. Where is he?'

'He's up at the apartment. That English guy kicked the crap out of the door, so it won't shut. We gotta preserve the scene until forensics turn up in the morning,' said Dev, taking a welcome swig of coffee.

'I thought I heard you guys. Ah, coffee. You're a life-saver, Ray,' said Mitch, poking his head out of the entrance to the building.

He grabbed the cup, then headed back towards the apartment. He paused in front of the steps and turned back to the street. Something had caught his eye.

'What's up, Mitch?' said Dev.

'What was the licence plate of that blue Toyota we were supposed to look out for?' said Mitch.

Ray picked up his notepad from the passenger seat. 'Echo, yankee, bravo, two, three, two, three.'

'That's it over there,' said Mitch.

Ray flicked his beams on full and got out of the car. The three officers put their coffee cups on the roof of the cop car and removed their guns and flashlights.

'Spread out, guys. I'll take the other side of the street. Mitch, you take this side. Dev, you go down the middle,' said Ray.

'Careful. This guy's armed and dangerous,' said Mitch.

They edged towards the Toyota guns raised and flashlights arcing over the doors and alleyways as they approached. Mitch reached the car first. He crouched and aimed his flashlight through the window.

'Nothing.'

They moved in sweeps, lighting up the shadows. All was dark; all was quiet.

Dev tried the driver's door. It popped open, and he searched the interior.

'Nothing in there. Let's call it in,' said Dev.

They relaxed, turning off the flashlights and holstering their guns, and walked back to the car with only a half-hearted glance back at the blue Toyota. Ray climbed back into the patrol car and picked up the radio.

Mitch popped his head through the window. 'You got my coffee, Ray?'

'Huh? No, they're on the roof.'

'Not anymore,' said Dev.

———

Snipe threw hot coffee into Dev's eyes. He yelled as Snipe passed him and grabbed Mitch by his throat, lifting him clean off his feet and slamming him onto the patrol car roof. He pulled the gun out of Mitch's holster and emptied six rounds through the window. Three of the bullets found their target and ripped through Ray's neck and cheek. Ray clutched his hands to his throat, eyes wide and scared as he desperately tried to stop the blood gushing out. Snipe didn't waste time. He put a bullet through Mitch's head and let his limp body slide to the ground. He turned and headed towards Dev. He was waving his gun around trying to focus through his scolded eyes. Snipe grinned and flipped his gun round, whacking the guy on the wrist with the butt. He heard the crunch of bones as Dev's gun clattered to the ground.

'Fucking feeble bastards, you Yanks,' said Snipe, and chuckled as he twisted the broken wrist, forcing Dev screaming to the ground.

Lights were coming on in the apartments along the street. Snipe knelt on the cop's chest while holding his wrist in a lock. He leered into bloodshot eyes.

'What happened here? How did you find this place?' he growled. The noise was soft and low. Dev squirmed under him and gasped.

'Aargh. O'Hanlin's phone... they tracked her phone... English guy.'

'What English guy?' said Snipe, raising his voice.

'I'm not sure... Pearson. David, no... Danny. Danny Pearson,'

Snipe felt the heat in his face as he lost control, raining punches into the man's head.

'Bastard fucking Pearson!'

He got up and unloaded the remaining rounds from the gun into Dev. He twitched for a moment as Snipe checked his surroundings. Snipe picked up Dev's loaded gun and fired through several apartment windows. The occupants darted out of sight. He breathed deeply to get his rage under control, then walked casually into the darkness of the alley that ran behind the apartment buildings. The approaching sirens grew louder with every second. Breaking into a run, Snipe followed the alley across two streets and emerged opposite a large twenty-four-hour supermarket. In the car park, a man in his mid- twenties, a sharp-suited professional type, was loading shopping bags into the back of his Mercedes. Snipe slowed to a casual walk and moved up behind him. He knocked him into the boot with one punch. Just to make sure, he leaned in and punched him again until the guy was still. He grabbed the keys from the ground, shut the boot and got in front of the wheel. He sat for a while thinking through his options. They had Spider's girlfriend, but she didn't know Spider or Marcus's location. He looked in the mirror. Two police cars screamed past, sirens wailing. If he turned on the girl's phone, they'd get his location. They either had—or would have—her phone records soon and would track Spider's mobile shortly after.

Fuck it. Gotta force things forward.

He pulled out the girl's phone and turned it on. After five rings, a nervous voice answered.

'Hello, Lisa,' said Spider.

'No, Cockroach, it's me,' said Snipe. A loud groan and thumping sound came from the boot of the car. 'That's her in the boot, arse-wipe. Now meet me in the Toys R Us car park down the road from your Batcave in half an hour, and you can say hello.'

He hung up and turned the phone off. The noise from the boot became louder. 'Jesus, what've I gotta do to get some fucking peace and quiet around here?'

Climbing out, Snipe moved to the back of the car and tapped the boot. 'Hey, buddy, you locked in there?'

'Help! Please. Somebody jumped me and locked me in,' came the muffled reply.

'Hold tight, me old mate. I'll get you out in a jiffy.'

Snipe looked around and a grin spread across his face. He spotted what he was looking for and trotted over to a bin. Seconds later he was opening the boot.

'Blimey, mate, what happened to you?' Snipe went as if to take the guy's hand and stabbed him with a broken beer bottle. He stood back as arterial blood erupted from the man's neck and grinned again. When the blood pressure had dropped and the flow had died to no more than a trickle, he slammed the trunk shut and returned to the driver's seat.

Firing up the engine he drove slowly out of the car park.

CHAPTER 47

Marcus sat in a booth in the shiny aluminium diner overlooking the bay. He sipped his coffee as he surveyed the old repair shop housing his servers and PCs some sixty metres away. Turning back to his laptop, he time-lapsed through the previous night's camera feeds. No activity around the building. He clicked onto the live feeds. Nothing there either. He looked at the building again. Something nagged as he clicked the feed covering the Mobil gas station and the large car park behind. He reached midnight, then forwarded the footage a minute at a time until he was watching a tatty blue Toyota turn into the car park entrance just past the petrol station. It reappeared from behind the neon lights of the forecourt and drove across the empty car park, stopping to face the shutter doors of the repair shop. Its lights went off. It remained stationary for eight minutes, then the lights came back on and it drove off. Marcus clicked forward to 2.45 a.m. and found what was bothering him: a silver Mercedes followed the same route as the Toyota, parking in the same place. It stayed for five minutes before driving away. He took a still and expanded it but couldn't make out the car's occupants. Unnerved, he checked the live feeds again, pleased that the only change was the image of Shane approaching the side door and unlocking it. The internal camera displayed him booting up a row of PCs. Marcus shut down the laptop and patted the holstered gun tucked under his jacket. He left the diner and strolled towards the old garage, scanning the surroundings as he went. No parked-up telecoms or work vans that could be a surveillance team. No mysterious joggers or men with hats and dark glasses sitting on benches, reading papers. No blue Toyotas or silver Mercedes either. Still rattled, he took a last look around before entering the repair shop.

'Where is the elusive Spider this morning?' Marcus said to Shane.

'Dunno. I heard his phone go early this morning. I guess he went to Lisa's mum's,' said Shane sheepishly.

'Hmm, change of plan, Shane. You and I are going to finish prepping and move the attack to today.'

Marcus turned on all the machines. Fans whirred and hard drives clicked.

'What? How? We can't. We need Spider,' said Shane.

'We can, and we will. If Spider doesn't show, you can have his share. What you do with it is your concern. Give it to Spider, keep it, I don't care, but the attack will be today... as soon as possible. So, let's get to work,' said Marcus calmly, forcing himself to smile.

Shane seemed to settle, and he got back to the computers. Marcus went through to the reception area and looked through a small circle etched in the whitewash. He surveyed the petrol station and car park before turning to look through another circle with a view past the funfair. Satisfied he wasn't under surveillance by the authorities or Snipe and Ramirez, he raised his phone. For the briefest moment, his hands shook with the underlying tension. He regained his composure and tapped in a number.

'Hi, this is Terence Blake. I have a private jet chartered for tomorrow evening to Buenos Aires... yes, just one passenger, but I need to bring the charter forward to tonight... yes, I understand there will be an additional charge. No problem... thank you. I will see you tonight.'

Marcus hung up, taking a deep breath. He made a second call.

'Darnel, it's Marcus. Are you ready, my brother?'

'Yes, we are ready and awaiting your instruction.'

'I am moving my plans forward. Today, America will fall to its knees. The

opportunity to hurt the UK and its corrupt government will soon present itself. Tomaz is set to get you access. Be patient, brother. Vengeance is coming. I will call you soon.'

Marcus hung up and peered through the whitewashed window one last time before returning to the server room.

CHAPTER 48

On the thirty-sixth floor of the FBI building, Danny slouched in his chair. Accompanying him were the rest of the team and fifteen FBI and Homeland Security staff. Fallen led the debrief on the previous day's events, clearly pleased with the progress they'd made but annoyed that the UK team had taken matters into their own hands. He reminded Paul and Edward that their team were to assist in an observational capacity only. Fallen went on to co-ordinate the manhunt for Marcus Tenby, Nicholas Snipe and Andrew Pitt. Lisa O'Hanlin's phone had been turned on in the early hours, making a call to Pitt. They had traced both phones to the Brooklyn Bay area before going dead at 3.05 a.m. Pitt's call records were in and being looked at. They were trying to find Pitt's friend, Shane Wallace. The final item on the agenda was the disappearance of a white male in his mid-twenties by the name of Lee Townsend, and his silver Mercedes GLA 200. He was last seen at a supermarket, only half a mile from where the police officers were murdered. As Fallen wrapped up the meeting, Danny rubbed his head. His nose had split and there were purple and black bags under his eyes from Ramirez's headbutt. He excused himself for the day and no one challenged him. In the back of the taxi, he brooded over Snipe. Dangerous and on the loose. He couldn't allow him to get away with the lives he'd destroyed.

Fuck it.

'Change of plan, mate. Can you take me down to the Brooklyn Bay area?'

'Sure thing, buddy,' said the taxi driver.

Danny's headache faded and his mood lifted as he took in the sights of the iconic bridge.

A short drive later they pulled off Belt Parkway. Danny asked the driver to drop him off by the Toys R Us store. It was in the centre of a mile-wide area they'd tracked Lisa and Spider's phones to before they'd gone dead. He paid the driver and received another, 'Have a nice day.'

Smiling Danny did a three-sixty, and cleared his head with a walk along the shoreline.

..

CHAPTER 49

Marcus looked through the circle in the whitewashed glass, scanning everything that moved. His nerves were fraying and his hands tremored constantly; it was barely noticeable, but there nevertheless. He'd been checking every thirty minutes but still couldn't see anything that looked out of place. Taking a deep breath he walked calmly through to the server room.

'Shane, status,' he commanded.

'Err, we've got eight machines engaged with the back door entries. The other five should be ready within half an hour,' said Shane triumphantly.

'Excellent. That's all the major banks. How are the secondary virus machines looking?' he said, decidedly more confident now that his end game was in sight.

'Yep, they're ready to go as soon as the back doors are engaged.'

'Good, good. Half an hour for the back doors and forty-five minutes for the viruses to take root in the system. Twenty-five minutes for the transfer machines to clean out the accounts. An hour and forty minutes and you'll be a very rich man.'

Shane poked his head over the monitor and smiled.

'Have you heard from Spider?' Marcus said.

'No, I tried his and his girlfriend's mobiles. They're both off,' Shane said, concern rising in his voice.

'His loss, my friend. You have your exit out of the country arranged?'

'Yes, the contact you gave me is flying me to Brazil tomorrow. I have everything

with me and won't be going home again. I'll crash in a hotel tonight.' 'Good. Tomorrow a new life awaits you.'

CHAPTER 50

C heering and applause rippled across the room and a beaming Scott bowed before his audience. MSI Software was back online and T.A. Leamings had been restored to full working order. MD Stephen Price and manager Phillip Gotts stepped forward and shook Scott's hand.

'Amazing. Thank you, Mr Miller. You've saved our necks,' said Price.

'My pleasure, old boy. And my new security software will block any future attacks,' he said smugly.

'Yes, sterling work, Mr Miller. When will the network go live?' said Gotts.

'Already has in the UK, Mr Gotts. And the US signed up last night. They should be going online as we speak. I have meetings with the countries that share the same banking software throughout the day and should have the whole community online and protected by the end of tomorrow.'

Scott checked his watch.

'I'm afraid I have to go, gentlemen. Meetings and all

that. Oh and thank you both for the swift payment for services rendered.'

Scott shook their hands again then walked awkwardly out of the building on his plastered leg and crutches, straight into a waiting car.

'Afternoon, Arthur. The Bank of England, please,' said Scott, smiling at the eyes looking back at him in the mirror.

'Busy day, sir?' Arthur said politely.

'Yes, old boy. I've got a video conference call with the financial bigwigs of five countries in a couple of hours. I'll definitely be ready for a pint or two after that one,' said Scott, fishing his phone out of his pocket.

'Well, just let me know, sir. Mr Gotts said to take you wherever you want to go.'

'Top man, thank you. Can I have a little privacy, please?'

Arthur nodded and pressed a button. The glass divider slid up between the front and back of the limousine.

Scott called the number and waited.

———

'Scotty boy, just the man I wanted to hear from. How are you, mate?' said Danny, cheered instantly by the call.

'On top form, old chap, and looking forward to your return. I have a little surprise for you when you get back,' said Scott.

'Oh yeah? What's that then? It's not my birthday.'

'If I told you, it wouldn't be a surprise, would it? You'll just have to wait until you get back.'

'Okay, okay. How's the banking stuff going? You got Leamings working yet?'

'All done. And thanks to you, I'm set to be the number-one security software provider for every financial institution in the world. I'm live in the UK and going live in the US as we speak,' said Scott triumphantly.

'Sod the Rose and Crown. It's lunch at the Granary when I'm back then,' said Danny with a chuckle.

'Absolutely, and I'll even throw in a dessert. But that's not why I'm calling. I found a large equipment purchase made by Marcus Tenby through a dummy company account in Belgium. Sixty-three thousand dollars' worth of Dell computers from Circuit City. I used the account details to get them to send me an invoice copy. And guess what? It's got a delivery address on it,' said Scott.

The enormity of Scott's revelation sunk in. 'Shit. Do you mean to say you've rendered Tenby's attack useless *and* you know where his is?'

'Yes, the American systems are going online now. And, yes, as long as Tenby is at Unit 5, Bay Forty-First Street, Brooklyn. Google says it used to be a garage called Bay Motors, which closed nearly three years ago,' said Scott.

'I'm stunned, mate. I've gotta go. Bad guys to catch. I'll see you when I get back,' said Danny.

He hung up and waved the waitress over, noting the name on her badge.

'Wendy, could you tell me where Bay Forty-First Street is?'

She pointed. 'Yes, darlin'. It's just over there, past the Mobil petrol station.'

'Is that Bay Motors next to it by the marina?' said Danny.

'Yep, that's it. You looking for the blond-haired guy with a crew cut?'

'Err, well, yes,' he said, taken by surprise.

He held out his phone with the picture of Tenby as Blake. 'This guy.'

'Yes, that's him, honey. Comes in here every morning

for coffee. Just stares at his cell or the repair shop for a half-hour before wandering over there,' she said.

'Thank you, Wendy.' Danny paid for the coffee and gave her a twenty-dollar tip.

He stepped outside, his features hardened and like a hunter zeroing in on its prey he stared at the old Bay Motors building in the distance.

CHAPTER 51

Shane's head appeared above the monitor. 'All the secondaries are engaged with the mainframe.'

'Good. Start the access program. Let's crash and transfer all the accounts,' said Marcus.

The enormous money transfers would bounce around the world, making them impossible to follow. One by one, access screens appeared. Shane grinned while Marcus reached towards the keyboard to begin the transfer on the first monitor.

The screen went blank.

He tapped the keys to refresh the display.

Another screen went down.

Marcus scanned the room. The monitors were dying in front of his eyes. Only three computers remained online. Marcus and Shane looked at each other in disbelief. The blank screens came to life, and a message started loading painfully slowly, one line at a time, creeping down from the top in green-screen like the first computers in the eighties.

Enraged, Marcus picked up a computer and launched it off the table. Its attached monitor and keyboard clattered to the floor after it. Shane jumped, and his expression turned to shock as he looked at the message: *Malicious software protection by Miller Software Inc. Your IP and server location have been tracked and reported to the authorities. Have a nice day.*

Marcus charged towards the four PCs still showing an access page.

'Shane get over here. We have to get everything out of these four banks before we lose access.'

His fingers moved at a frantic pace. Shane worked on the PC next to him. As Marcus keyed in the final command, the third monitor went blank.

'The other one. Get on the other one,' Marcus yelled.

———

Danny entered the shop of the Mobil petrol station. Pretending to browse, he peered out the side window. The old Bay Motors building was visible through a gap behind a tanker refuelling. Phone to his ear, he looked across at the shuttered doors and the marina behind the building.

'Paul, put Fallen on.'

The phone went quiet for a few seconds, then Fallen spoke.

'Danny, what's going on?' His irritation was clear.

'Get your men to the old Bay Motors garage on Bay Forty-First Street, Brooklyn, ASAP. It's Tenby's server base and I'm fairly sure he's in there now.'

'We're on our way. Do not engage, understand? Just stay back and call me if anyone leaves.'

Danny heard Fallen barking orders then he came back on the line.

'Stay back and observe.'

The line went dead.

Danny pocketed the phone as a silver flash in the

corner of his eye caught his attention. He looked towards the car park. A silver Mercedes parked up thirty metres behind the gas station. The door opened and the car rocked as a massive figure climbed out. Danny froze in disbelief as Snipe pulled out a gun and walked calmly towards the repair shop. Then he lost sight of him, the tanker obscuring his view.

'Shit.'

Exiting the shop he skirted around the front, past the pumps. He tucked himself behind the tanker and peeped his head around. Snipe put the gun on the ground and stooped to pick the lock on the whitewashed reception door. Ten seconds later he was in. Danny sprinted across the forecourt and road that ran alongside the repair shop and planted his back against the wall beside the reception door.

Shit fucking shit.

He listened for any sirens approaching. Nothing. Then a muffled scream came from within the building.

Fuck it.

He slipped through the door into the reception area. A large Formica desk stood at the far end, other than that, it was empty. Someone was whimpering beyond the door to the workshop, and Snipe barked angrily at someone, presumably Tenby. Danny kept low and tested the door, pushing it open a millimetre at a time until he could slide through the gap. A row of PCs and a server cabinet covered him as he entered. Behind the cabinet, Shane lay doubled-up on the floor in the middle of the room. He rolled around moaning. Next to him Snipe pointed a gun at Tenby.

'You screwed us over and now I want the money, all of it, or I'm gonna rip you apart slowly,' Snipe growled.

'Nicholas, my friend, I can get you your money but not

the riches we hoped for. We have been blocked by Scott Miller. Yes, the man you were supposed to have killed. So, I fear it is me who's been ripped off. I could only get into one bank and was blocked before I could transfer all their funds,' said Tenby.

'Don't fucking *my friend* me, you wanker. Just transfer the money before I—' Snipe cocked his head to one side at the faint sound of approaching sirens. 'Do it now!' he shouted.

As he turned, Danny launched himself off a table in a flying tackle, a monitor in his raised arms. As he came down, he slammed it into Snipe's forehead. Glass and plastic flew in all directions as it bent round his head. Snipe slumped into a table, sending PCs clattering to the floor. Danny rolled to one side and spotted Tenby ducking behind a server cabinet. He turned his attention back to Snipe and went in for the attack. Before he got there, Snipe exploded upright and started punching him in the chest. The powerful blows sent him backwards over the table. More PCs and monitors went flying. He rolled through the pain behind a server cabinet, just missing a hail of bullets unleashed from Snipe's gun. Sparks and smoke fizzed above his head as shots ripped through the switches in the cabinet. The sirens grew louder and Snipe bolted for the door. Danny leapt over the tables and headed for the server cabinet Tenby had crawled behind. He was met by an open door to the marina beyond.

Tenby was nowhere to be seen.

CHAPTER 52

D anny wasted no time. He set off after Snipe as shots, sirens, and screeching tyres echoed from outside. Two cop cars were positioned sideways on the road. Bullet holes riddled their windscreens. One officer was pulling his injured colleague to cover. Danny looked over at the petrol station. Snipe punched out the tanker driver and climbed into the cab. He broke into a sprint and reached the back of the tanker just as Snipe ground it into gear. It lurched forward. Danny leapt for the rear ladder as it moved off and got a hand-hold. The fuel pipe ripped off the coupling and a fountain of fuel sprayed across the forecourt from the back of the tanker. He hung, feet dragging along the road, then pulled himself onto the ladder and climbed to the roof. The tanker thundered along the road, following the bay.

A line of FBI and police cars dropped in behind it, snaking over the slippery fuel as it pumped out over the tarmac. Danny inched along the walkway on top of the tanker and dropped into the gap behind the cab. Taking hold of the grab bar on the back of the cab, he swung out wide, hurling a left fist through the open driver's-side window and connecting hard with Snipe's cheek. The tanker swung to one side, bounced up the kerb, then slid back onto the road. Snipe turned to face Danny with insanity in his eyes as he grinned widely. He lurched the tanker hard to the left. Danny glanced forward in time to see an impending collision with a parked delivery van. He swung back behind the cab just as the tanker side-swiped the van. The vehicles bounced off each other in a scream of scraping metal. Fragments of glass and plastic from the mirrors exploded from the impact. Danny looked back. The hose was still pumping fuel onto the road while a parade of cars gave chase. He edged across to the passenger-side grab-rail and felt around with his right hand for the door handle. With a one-two-three count he yanked the door open and swung himself into the cab. Snipe pulled his gun, forcing Danny to launch himself against the windscreen and push Snipe's wrist away as he squeezed off a couple of rounds. The sound was deafening and his ears rang as the shots blew out the passenger window.

Holding Snipe's gun arm back with one hand, he punched him in the kidneys with the other. It was like hitting a brick wall. Snipe pushed Danny's arm slowly back, twisting the gun towards his face. Danny headbutted the bridge of Snipe's nose. The cartilage collapsed on impact and Snipe's face contorted as blood teemed from his nose and his eyes streamed. Danny grabbed the gun and twisted it out of his hand. As he turned the gun on Snipe a boot planted in his chest, kicking him out through the passenger door. He swayed wildly but hooked an arm through the windowless doorframe. Turning his attention forward, Snipe saw the road bending sharply right with the glistened bay beyond it. He heaved on the steering wheel, fighting to make the corner. The tanker squealed and started to jack-knife before turning over. It flung Danny over a hedge and into the swimming pool of a bay-front holiday home.

Metal met tarmac, igniting the trailing fuel. A jet of flame accelerated towards the tanker and away down the road they'd come from. The chasing cars swerved out of its path, their wheels alight for a few moments until the fuel burnt off. The flames caught up with the tanker as it slid through the twin metal crash barriers between the road and the bay. The explosion peeled the tanker open like a sardine tin and a forty-foot-high fireball erupted from the destruction. The tanker hit the water a second later and sunk, leaving only a burning fuel slick in its wake. The police and FBI cars screeched to a halt by the gap in the rails. The officers and agents cornered off the scene as they looked for signs of Snipe in the water. Danny had pulled himself out of the pool and lay on the lawn, breathing heavily. Paul and Tom ran across to him.

'You okay?' said Paul.

Danny dragged his soaking wet body upright. 'Snipe?'

Paul and Tom just shook their heads.

CHAPTER 53

arcus ran along the wooden walkway and jumped into a small twin-engine speedboat. As he cast off the rope, he looked around. No one had followed him through the back door and no officers were looking down from the car park above. The powerful engines gurgled and popped. He rammed the throttle forward. The engine screamed and the boat zipped out of the small marina and into Gravesend Bay. When he'd put some distance between himself and dry land he looked back, catching sight of the tanker thundering out of the gas station, a line of cars in pursuit. He backed off the throttle and smiled as he cruised around Coney Island, then powered down and let the boat bob in the water like any other day-tripper. He flipped up one of the seat storage boxes, grabbed a large canvas sports bag, and unzipped it. Laptop, passport, wallet—check. Under the spare clothes sat a large roll of hundred-dollar bills and a Glock 19. He zipped the bag back up and stowed it, then glared across at the funfair as music and screams of delight carried across the water. Hatred burned in his gut. He kicked the engine on and headed for Rockaway Inlet and a small marina behind Floyd Bennett airfield.

After he'd moored up, he wandered over to the marina car park and an old Ford pickup. He reached into a bag of garden rubbish sitting between an old lawnmower and an assortment of rusty gardening tools, pulled out the keys, and unlocked the door. He climbed in behind the wheel and tapped his phone.

'Hello. This is Terence Blake. I believe you have a charter booked for me to Argentina. I'll be there in around forty minutes. Yes, thank you. I'll see you then.'

He pulled sedately onto Flatbush Avenue and headed for the airport.

CHAPTER 54

Danny and the team made their way back to the old Bay Motors building. Shane was being stretchered into an ambulance under armed guard. He had multiple fractures from where Snipe had beaten him with a fire extinguisher. Fallen paced up and down in front of the reception area, clearly in a foul mood after discovering that Tenby had slipped away. They had scrambled the coastguard helicopter, but it was a sunny day and small boats were strewn all around the bay. A report came in confirming that Scott's software had blocked all malicious attacks, apart from Citibank—Tenby had transferred forty-six million dollars before the software had gone live. That, and six million pounds still missing from Leamings, had been moved through a long chain of banks with tight client-confidentiality agreements or based in countries that wouldn't co-operate with an investigation from the West. The crime-scene investigators wanted them out of the way, so Fallen sent them back to the Hilton. Back at the hotel, Danny excused himself from the group and limped into the lift. He was a mess, his clothes ragged, his body covered in cuts and scrapes, and his hair all over the place from being literally dragged through a hedge backwards. His adrenaline had long since gone. He put one arm against the side and rested his head on the mirrored panel, utterly exhausted. He entered his room and emptied his still damp pockets on the desk. The screen of his phone was cracked and water trickled out of it. Throwing it down, he turned his attention to his soggy wallet. He pulled out the hundred or so dollars and his cards and driving licence. Three old photos came last—one of his mum and dad, one of Rob, and one of his late wife and son. He spread them out to dry with the other items and stared at them. After peeling off his wet clothes, he sat on the edge of the bed. A tear trickled down his cheek as he looked again at his wife and child. Wiping it away, he took out his iPad and clicked on FaceTime, suddenly desperate to talk to only one person in the world.

'Hello, stranger. How are—? Danny, your face. You look dreadful. Are you okay?' said Trisha.

'I'm fine. All the better for seeing you. I've missed you,' said Danny wearily.

'I miss you too. Are you sure you're okay? When are you coming home?'

'I'm fine, honest. It looks worse than it is. As for coming home, I imagine it'll be soon. The attack got stopped. Tenby got away and is probably out of the country by now. The rest of the bad guys are either dead or locked up so there's not much left for us to do.'

A smile crept onto his face and his spirits lifted as they talked. Danny didn't mention the knife fight with Ramirez, or Snipe and the tanker. He didn't want to over a long-distance call. Instead, they said their love you's, and he promised to call as soon as he bought a new phone. A long, hot shower loosened up his aching, bruised limbs. He shaved and dressed and went down to join the others for dinner.

As he entered the bar, Paul, Tom, Edward, Glen, and John clapped and cheered. 'What's all this for, guys? Tenby got away.'

'You need to learn not to be so hard on yourself. You stopped the bad guys, and with help from Scott, prevented a financial meltdown in the Western world. If that isn't an excuse for celebration, I don't know what is,' said Paul, passing him a beer.

Danny raised his glass and grinned. 'In that case, cheers!'

CHAPTER 55

At nine the following morning, Paul and Edward stood in front of the team in a large meeting room on the thirty-sixth floor of the FBI building. Danny, Tom, Glen and John slouched in their chairs with cans of energy drinks, coffee or orange juice. Despite the hangover, Danny felt better than he had the day before. Most of his pain had dulled to aching and stiffness. The lack of agents and national security personnel in the meeting intrigued him. Then Fallen entered followed by an army general.

'Gentlemen, this is General Dale Parnell. The general has come direct from the White House and would like to address you.'

The group sat up, their interest piqued.

'Good morning, gentlemen. First, I'd like to thank you and your colleagues on behalf of the president and the United States. Your tireless efforts undoubtedly averted unimaginable economic disasters for both our countries. We currently have every resource looking for Marcus Tenby. Intel gained from Shane Wallace suggests that

Tenby booked a private charter plane out of the country yesterday afternoon. The FBI questioned every charter company or pilot in New York state and found a booking with Walton Air Charter for Terence Blake to Buenos Aires, Argentina. The pilot stayed overnight and returned today. We've spoken to him and he's positively identified Tenby from photographs. This brings us to the purpose of this meeting. Last night, the president and the prime minister sat with their security councils to discuss the situation. They are in agreement—we cannot allow Marcus Tenby to get away with his terrorist activities in the USA and UK. We must recover the money he stole. Unfortunately, we cannot extradite Tenby. To do so would expose how close the United States came to financial ruin. That would open the floodgates for all our enemies and increase their cyber terrorism efforts. Our governments have a fragile relationship with Argentina, and we cannot risk a political meltdown by sending in agents to secure Tenby. We would like to enlist your help and contract Greenwood Security under the pretence of a personal-security detail. Your mission is to find and return Tenby to the USA to answer for his crimes. We have an agent in Buenos Aires trying to locate him, and we will organise transport for the extraction once you have apprehended the target. This will be a private mission and completely deniable in the event of failure.'

There was silence as the general's words sank in. Paul was the first to break it.

'I am happy with the proposal in principle, but I need to discuss this with my colleagues. I would also need a substantial deposit to cover contractual costs.'

'Of course, Mr Greenwood. I have been given complete authority to cover any operational costs and to equip you with whatever you need,' said General Parnell.

'In that case, if I could ask for a short break to talk to my men...'

'Certainly, we will reconvene in an hour,' the general said, walking towards the door, Fallen close behind.

'Excuse me, General. Do you have any news on the tanker driver, Nicholas Snipe?' said Danny.

'I'm afraid not, son. The divers said the cab was ripped apart and empty. The current is very strong there. His body was probably dragged out into the bay. We have the coastguard out looking but it's possible we'll never find him.'

The general gave a quick nod then left.

Paul stood and faced them. 'Okay guys. Your thoughts.'

'Yeah, I'm in,' said Tom.

'Me too,' said John.

Danny nodded.

'I wish me and Glen could join you, but we have to return to the MI6 headquarters,' said Edward.

'I understand, Edward,' said Paul. 'I'll be sorry to see both of you go. As for the rest of you, I'll make sure you're all very, very well paid for this little excursion.'

The group broke for coffee. Edward and Glen said their goodbyes and the rest of the team returned to the meeting room. A lean, dark-haired man with glasses joined the general and Fallen. He was dressed casually in jeans and a sweatshirt.

The general stepped forward. 'Okay, gentlemen, are we good?'

'Yes, we are in agreement,' said Paul.

'Excellent. Then we'll begin. This is Lucas Gonzalez. He's from Buenos Aires, grew up there, and knows the people and places like the back of his hand. He'll be posing as your client. We have you booked on a flight out of JFK later today. On arrival you'll be met by Agent Gaspar

Rodriguez. We have booked a large villa with a walled perimeter as your client's residence. Whatever you need—money, equipment, transport—just tell Mr Rodriguez and we'll get it to you. Any questions?' said General Parnell.

'What's your intended extraction plan?' said Danny.

'Simple and low risk. We have men in place who can give us access to a Federal Express cargo plane. All you have to do is tranquillise Tenby, crate him up, and ship him back to the US.'

Danny nodded his approval.

'Each of my men requires a non-refundable payment prior to leaving for Argentina. This is in addition to the operational payment to Greenwood Security,' said Paul.

'Certainly, Mr Greenwood. Give me the details, I'll make the call,' said the general, gesturing to a phone on the desk.

'Thank you,' said Paul.

As Paul and the general moved to the side of the room, Fallen came over and thanked them for their assistance then excused himself. Lucas introduced himself. He'd worked for Argentina's infamous secret police before falling in love with a US diplomat. They'd married and moved to the US, where the FBI had recruited him. Although small in stature, he bore the character and confidence of a larger man.

'Ah, Mr Pearson. A pleasure to meet you. I've been following your exploits over the past couple of weeks. I must say, you're looking well, considering,' he said.

'Hmm, I guess I've been very lucky, or maybe very unlucky depending on which way you look at it,' said Danny with a smile.

'Yes, I suppose it does,' Lucas said, grinning. 'Now, we must get ready for the journey. It's a long flight and I can brief you on the way.'

203

CHAPTER 56

ola Vetrano stood by her Renault Clio in a smart
black skirt suit and heels. She'd dressed up a little
more than usual as she waited to hand over the
keys in person. Two months ago, the handsome Toby
Birbeck had walked into the real-estate agency where she
worked and instructed her to purchase a property. With a
large bonus for fast completion on offer, Lola had pulled
out all the stops and today was payday. Earlier that morning, just over 3.5 million pounds had been transferred to
complete the exchange, and here she was, paperwork and
keys in hand. Glad of the cooler April breeze, she stood in
the sunshine waiting patiently in front of the electric gates
that secured this large ranch-style house in Belgrano,
Buenos Aires. A procession of black Land Cruisers moved
towards her. The three cars stopped in front of her and
armed security personnel exited the front and rear vehicles.
They scanned the surrounding area then opened the
middle car's rear door. Toby Birbeck climbed out. He was
dressed in a sharp tailored Armani suit and sunglasses. His
hair wasn't as long and wavy as when they'd first met and

his beard had turned to designer stubble, but his handsome Middle Eastern looks still shone through.

'Miss Vetrano, how lovely to see you again,' he said, taking her hand and leaning in to kiss her on the cheek.

She blushed. 'It's a pleasure to see you again, Mr Birbeck. Shall we?'

'Please,' he said, gesturing towards the gate.

Lola pulled a small fob out of a manila envelope and pressed it. The heavy gates slid smoothly open and four members of the security detail moved swiftly inside ahead of Birbeck and Lola.

Birbeck nodded then gestured Lola through the gate. The three vehicles passed them, and the gates closed gently behind.

They reached the front door.

'The keys to your new home,' said Lola, handing her client the keys. 'I hope you'll be very happy here.' She noticed a frown cross his face; it lasted only a second, but she'd caught it all the same.

'Thank you, Miss Vetrano. I'm sure I will. And as agreed, here is a gesture of my appreciation for all your help.'

'Thank you,' said Lola, taking the envelope trying to hide her delight at the money she knew lay within.

Birbeck opened the front door and stepped over to the beeping keypad. He tapped in the code written on the manila envelope Lola had given him, silencing it, then turned back to her.

'Thank you once again, Miss Vetrano. Miguel will escort you to your car.'

'Oh, err, yes, of course, Mr Birbeck. It's been a pleasure.'

———

Marcus moved to the security room and watched the gates shut behind her. A large screen displayed feeds from the house, the self-contained annexe, the security staff, the gardens and the outside wall.

Miguel came in. 'I will set up the schedules and provisions for the staff, Mr Birbeck. Is there anything else I can do for you?'

'Not for the moment, Miguel. The domestic help will be here at 2.00 p.m. and the interior designer shortly after with the furniture delivery. I trust you will check them in and out,' said Marcus, watching as one of the other staff brought his bags from the car.

'Yes, Mr Birbeck,' said Miguel.

Marcus went into the hall and wheeled his bags to his office. A screen in the corner duplicated the security feed. On the wall were rows of network TV and satellite outlets. He opened his bags and removed two laptops, setting them on the beautiful handcrafted hardwood desk. He connected the power and internet cables to wall plates and the screens lit up. Then he typed Dinash1953 into the login window and Shada1991 for the password. The first was his father's name and year of birth. The second was his mother's name and the year they'd been killed in the American air strike.

He sat in the leather chair. A man with so many names...

The laptop screens finished loading and he stared, steely-eyed. Underneath his calm exterior he was in turmoil—a combination of fury, hatred, and the despair of failure. Yes, he had money. But it had never been about that. He'd always had money. He'd earned it, stolen it or convinced people to give it to him. Money had never been a problem. It was twenty-seven years of planning the financial downfall of America— only to have failed—that was tearing him apart. Damn Scott Miller and Danny Pearson. Forcing himself to focus, he opened an encryption program and typed: *Brother Darnel, my mission has failed. The American and English infidels have taken Akbar, Barzan and Kadah from us. They are with the faith now and bask in the glory of Allah. Your wait is over. I order you to proceed with our plans. The targets have changed in our favour. The prime minister will join the American president to announce a new anti-terrorism collaboration. On the 24th at 12.30 p.m. we will take our revenge and destroy the leaders of the Western world. You have all the details and the equipment you need. Tomaz will contact you with access to the venue for the device. It must be in position by the 22nd, before the security services do their sweeps. Good luck, my brother, you will be immortalised in the history books.*

Pressing send he sat back in the chair, exhaling deeply. Despite sacrificing many pawns and losing some key pieces in his game of revenge, checkmate was still obtainable. He typed a second message into the encryption program: *Tomaz, your loyalty is about to be rewarded. I attach a contact for Darnel. Meet him and his friends. You must get them into the plant room by the 22nd. They will do the rest.* He sent the message, logged out, and closed the lids of both laptops. Feeling calmer, he studied the CCTV and watched as the domestic staff and a delivery lorry were escorted through the gates. Charisma back on display, he walked to the front door and greeted them.

'Ladies, welcome. Miguel has your duty schedules. I hope you will be very happy working here,' he said to the staff as they passed, nodding and smiling.

'Through here, gentlemen. Let's make this place a home.' He waved in the delivery men and smiled warmly as they showed the interior designer in.

CHAPTER 57

The rhythmic hum of the aeroplane's engines was strangely comforting. Danny had slept soundly for the entire flight, only waking when the sound changed, and the plane angled downwards for the descent into San Fernando Airport, Buenos Aires. Baggage and passport control were uneventful. Lucas led the way into the arrivals hall. He was greeted with a warm handshake from a short Argentinian. Gaspar Rodriguez, Danny presumed. The agent passed Lucas and greeted the team.

'Welcome, welcome. I am Gaspar. So very pleased to meet you. If you would like to follow me, I have arranged transport to our villa.'

The group moved through the airport and out into the hot Argentinian sunshine where a minibus was waiting for them. They drove through the bustling city and out to a wealthy suburb before turning into the drive of a large villa. Lucas paid the driver as Gaspar beckoned them inside.

'This way, *caballeros*. Very nice, no? Best American

dollar can buy my friends.' They entered the pristine hall of the villa.

'Please pick a room and drop your *pantalon*, err, bags, and join me in the living room,' he said, then launched into a conversation of indecipherably fast Spanish with Lucas.

The villa was modern and immaculately clean. Danny broke away from the others and found a big, bright, double bedroom that overlooked the lush green garden. The lawn, borders, and flower beds were as well maintained as the building. His pocket buzzed. Danny pulled out his new mobile and smiled at the screen.

Hope you had a good flight. I miss you. Don't look at any strange women. Love, Trish xx. He typed slowly with his thumbs. *Slept the whole flight. Miss you too. Don't worry—I'll only talk to women who aren't strange. Be home in no time. Love you xx.* Then he pocketed the phone and joined the others in the living room.

The FBI's faith in Gaspar turned out to be well deserved; he had contacts throughout the city—police, traffic, government, every cafe, estate agent and newsagent. Gaspar had spread the files out on the table: three possible leads on Marcus Tenby. The first was from Executive Air, whose private charter to Cape Town two days from now included a passenger described as Middle Eastern and of approximately Tenby's height and build. He was booked into the penthouse suite of the Park Hyatt Hotel under the name Akram Farooq. The second lead had come from an interior designer, Carla Ortiz. Her client had bought a large property a few months earlier and commissioned her services for his whole house, no expense spared. He'd arrived at the same time as Tenby and fitted the description. Third was the letting agent Gaspar had rented their villa from. Three Arabic IT consultants had rented a villa half a mile from their location. At least one of them was a match for Tenby, and they'd been throwing large amounts of money around the city.

Reconnaissance would start in the morning with the hotel.

CHAPTER 58

D arnel exited Charing Cross Tube station and went up the stairs and into the throng of tourists taking photos of Nelson's Column and the black lion statues at its base. He barged past, attracting some mutters in Chinese as he knocked them, and their selfie sticks off-balance. He crossed the road and turned down Whitehall. A hundred metres down he paused outside McDonald's. The grey London drizzle seeped through his clothes as he stared in the direction of the Foreign Office. He ignored the chill and the rain as he imagined the president and prime minister standing in front of their podiums as the bomb went off. The tall, dark, twenty-seven year old Somalian had been in Britain since he'd stowed away on a boat at the age of fifteen. He'd claimed asylum and been fostered by a family in London. After attending Barzan Naser's mosque he'd become one of his most devout followers, ready and willing to serve The Faith however he could. Entering McDonald's Darnel ordered a coffee. As he waited he glanced across the seating area, easily spotting the nervous Tomaz from his maintenance uniform and

211

security pass. He took his drink and walked confidently over. Sitting down opposite Tomaz, he offered a smile and a nod.

'Try to look more relaxed, brother,' said Darnel.

'Sorry,' Tomaz replied.

'You have the plan to get us in?'

'Yes, the maintenance manager will be off for the next few days, courtesy of a chemistry-graduate friend of mine. His packed lunch will keep him on the toilet for at least forty-eight hours. As maintenance supervisor, I'll be in charge until he's back. I will cause a fault in the heating to the Grand Reception Room of the Locarno Suite tonight. At midday tomorrow, bring your van to the side entrance of the Foreign Office. Security will be expecting you and I'll sign you in to the building,' said Tomaz, finishing his Big Mac.

'Good. Tomorrow at midday.' Darnel rose from his seat and walked out into the drizzle.

Tomaz finished his drink and sat shaking slightly as the magnitude of his involvement hit him. Shaking it off, he left McDonald's and took the short walk back down White-hall to the Foreign Office. He passed through security with a wave as he'd done every day for the last three years and entered the building without a second glance.

CHAPTER 59

Gaspar returned from the check-in desk at the Park Hyatt with a wide grin on his face.

'Heads up. What's he so happy about?' said Tom.

'Yes, he's still in the penthouse. Room service took him breakfast an hour ago. So, let's go, yes?' said Gaspar.

'Okay, but tell us why you're grinning first,' said Danny.

'Ah, the gorgeous Gabriella on reception,' said Gaspar, grinning wider as he held up a slip of paper with a phone number written on it.

'Enough. Let's go,' said Lucas, heading for the lifts.

There was something about Lucas that Danny couldn't put his finger on, an uneasy feeling. Paul and John took watch in reception while the others went up to the top floor. Danny picked the lock on the chambermaid's cupboard, and Lucas and Gaspar slipped inside. After checking the coast was clear, he and Tom moved along the corridor to the door marked *Staff Only*. Tom covered Danny while he worked on the lock. Within seconds, they were in. A passage led into a large plant room. They changed into boiler suits, caps and shades, stuffed their disregarded clothes into rucksacks, then headed up the stairs and out onto the roof.

'Alpha Team in position one,' said Danny though his throat mic.

'Lobby's all quiet,' said Paul in his earpiece.

Lucas and Gaspar had changed into hotel uniforms. Lucas had loaded a tranquilliser dart into a small air gun and tucked it into a laundry cart. They wheeled it into the hall and moved slowly towards the penthouse suite.

'Delta Team moving into position now,' said Lucas a second later.

'Alpha Team in position two. Ready to lower. Delta Team, stand by for a positive ID,' said Danny.

Tom flicked the switch, lowering the window cleaner cradle down the outside of the hotel and stopping by the penthouse living-room window. Tom soaped up the glass while Danny looked through the smear. A figure walked to the bedroom and out of sight. His build matched Tenby's.

'Delta Team, stand by. Suspect spotted. Waiting for a positive ID,' said Danny calmly as he squeegeed the soap away.

The suspect came back into the living room area but turned to look in the mirror before Danny could get a look at him.

'The mirror. I saw his face. I think it's him,' said Tom.

'Are you sure, Tom?' said Danny, seeing the apartment door inch open and a tranquilliser gun being lined up through the gap.

'Tom, are you sure?'

'I think—'

The suspect turned and glanced briefly at the window.

'Abort. Abort. It's not him. I repeat, it's not him,'

Danny said urgently, feeling the seconds drag until the apartment door gently closed. Whizzing the squeegee across the window, he looked at the man chatting on his mobile, completely unaware of how close he'd come to being dumped in a laundry cart and shipped back to the USA in a FedEx crate.

He flicked the controls, and the cradle moved smoothly back up to the roof.

Ten minutes later the team walked out of the hotel with nobody any the wiser. They crossed the street and headed into a cafe.

'Okay, Gaspar, who's next—the IT consultants or the interior designer's lead?' said Danny, devouring a pastry.

'Ah, the IT *consultores*, *si*. They are closest and have no security or wall, so should be easy to get a positive *identificación*, err, identification,' Gaspar said.

'That's fine, mate,' said Tom to the smiling Argentinian.

———

As Danny, Paul, Gaspar and Lucas drove past the villa in one of the two unremarkable cars they'd hired that morning, the three businessmen were standing by a black Mercedes in the drive, clearly identifiable by the suits, briefcases and laptop bags. Obviously off to some meeting in the city. None looked particularly like Tenby. They turned the next corner and met John and Tom in the other car. The team had an impromptu meeting and agreed to do a drive-by reconnaissance of the ranch house. The half-hour drive took them into the affluent Belgrano area. The buildings became grander. The plush apartments were followed by houses surrounded with spike-topped walls, heavy electric gates, CCTV cameras and security alarms.

The suspect's ranch-style house was no exception. Cameras sat atop the high wall to monitor the perimeter, and armed security personnel guarded the gate. Danny's senses tingled as they passed slow enough to get a good look but fast enough not to draw attention.

'How sure was Ortiz about the appearance match?' said Danny to Gaspar.

'I show her the pictures of Tenby with longer hair and beard and as Terence Blake, clean-shaven and short blonde hair. The man is called Toby Birbeck and has short, dark hair and stubbly beard now, but when she first met him, he looked like the photo of Tenby,' said Gaspar.

'He's in there—I can feel it,' said Danny, glancing back at the security staff on the gate. 'I need the phone and broadband information for that address, Gaspar. Can you get it?'

'Okay. I need to make some calls. I have *contacto* in Telecom Argentina. We go back to villa, yes?' said Gaspar to Lucas in the driving seat.

'What's the plan?' said Paul.

'If I can get the info, I'll get Scott to hack into the camera system. See if we can get a positive ID.'

Paul nodded.

CHAPTER 60

A blue Ford Transit turned into the access road leading to a small courtyard at the Foreign Office. It pulled to a halt by the barrier and security hut. *M&K Air Conditioning and Heating* decals had been sign-written onto the bodywork. Darnel, Spencer and Omar sat in the cab. The company logo adorned their blue boiler suits. Darnel leaned out the driver's-side window and called to the security guard.

'Hi, mate. Got a call-out for a Tomaz Grinzski about a faulty heating system in the Grand Reception Room.'

The security guard rifled through his paperwork.

'Okay, come through and park in bay three. Give the van keys to the guard on the door and head for the waiting room.'

Darnel did as instructed. They were met by two security guards and a sniffer dog.

'This will just take a minute,' said the security guard, waving them through to the small room.

'Hey, mate, you won't find any drugs in there!' said Darnel, grinning.

217

'It's an explosives dog, sir. Just routine. Please have a seat,' said the guard with no hint of humour.

As soon as they were alone, their faces fell. The sound of the panel doors sliding open sent chills down their spines. One guard checked the tools and pipes, then moved to the cabin. The second went around the van with a mirror on a stick, checking the underside. The dog jumped in the back of the van, sniffing a Viessmann boiler-parts box before leaping out the back and into the cab. It sniffed around for a moment then jumped out and sat by its keeper's side. Satisfied, the guards closed the van doors. The dog and its handler wandered off to the security hut. The other guard went into the waiting room where the three men were trying to look as relaxed as possible.

'Okay, gentlemen, I'll just give Tomaz Grinzski a call and he'll come and escort you. As you don't have registered security clearance, Mr Grinzski will have to stay with you at all times. If you can just sign the visitors log and put a badge on, I'll be back in a minute.'

The guard left and picked up the phone in the room opposite. After a couple of minutes, footsteps came down the corridor. They heard Tomaz greeting the guard before poking his head round the waiting-room door.

'Good morning, gentlemen. If you would like to load all your tools onto one of the trolleys outside, I'll take you up to the Grand Reception Room,' he said.

The loaded trolley squeaked and rattled through the back corridors. Back in the building's heyday, these corridors would have been bustling with serving staff attending to government officials, lords and ladies, and visiting dignitaries. Now they were empty, the walls plain and scuffed, the floor bare concrete. The cleaners, serving staff and suited maître d's nodded as Tomaz greeted them all by name as they passed through a seemingly endless number of heavy fire doors. They reached a tiny service lift shoe-horned behind the stairwell. One floor up, they exited, following Tomaz as he led them to a landing next to the Grand Reception Room. Darnel, although grimly focused on his mission, couldn't help but stare at the grandeur, astounded by the ornate mouldings and beautiful painted ceilings. Familiarity had made Tomaz oblivious. He turned a corner and opened a hidden door in the wall revealing a plant and boiler room. The trolley went first, then they followed and closed the door behind them. The heat in the room was oppressive. Tomaz immediately dropped his convivial facade.

'The hot-air duct feeding the Grand Reception Room is over there. The service hatch is above it.' He pointed to the large square metal ducting. It went up the wall and across the ceiling, then disappeared into the wall. Halfway across was a steel- hinged inspection hatch secured with wing nuts at the top.

Tomaz grabbed a stepladder stowed at the rear of the room.

'Hurry, please. The sooner this is done the better,' he said. Sweat beaded on his forehead.

Sweating profusely, Darnel and Omar opened the large Viessmann box, lifted out the two-foot-long device, and placed it gently on the floor. The two bright-yellow cylinders were clamped together like divers' breathing apparatus. The cylinders were stencilled with Cyrillic script and a large stamp: *CY17*. At one end, they had paired a motorised valve and a timer with a mobile phone. Spencer activated the phone and then slid it into the ducting. The door swung open as Spencer was closing the hatch.

'Excuse me, gentlemen, can I ask what you're doing here?' said the security guard.

'Hi, Kevin. These guys are just fixing the heating

system for the hall,' said Tomaz, appearing from behind a boiler.

'Oh, Tomaz, I didn't see you there. Who called this in?' said Kevin, eying the men cautiously.

'I did. Douglas is off sick so it's down to me to sort the heating in the Grand Reception Room. It's all in the maintenance log.'

Kevin said nothing for a minute as he looked at the empty box, then at Spencer up the steps, screwing the hatch shut.

'Gents, I just need to ask you what was in the box and what's behind that hatch,' said Kevin, with one hand poised over the two-way radio on his lapel. From twenty years in the Metropolitan Police prior to working at the Foreign Office, Kevin had an instinct when something wasn't right.

'Come on, Kevin. Just let the guys get on with their work,' said Tomaz moving between him and the others.

'Step back, please, Tomaz. I need to see what's in that duct.' Kevin moved around him.

'It's okay—it's just a fan motor. Come here and I'll show you,' said Darnel calmly.

Kevin moved forward and peered into the box. A confused look spread across his face as he stared at the empty interior. He looked up questioningly and Darnel pulled his hand away from the radio and punched a large screwdriver into his chest. He withdrew it, then thrust it up under Kevin's chin, right up to the handle, piercing his brain. Keven dropped like a stone.

'What have you done?' said Tomaz. 'What the hell have you done? It's all over. We've had it.'

Spencer and Omar looked at each other, their faces draining of colour, mouths open in silent shock. Darnel grabbed Tomaz by the collar. 'Shut up and calm down.

This changes nothing. You two get the plastic out of the box and wrap him up in it. We'll put him in the box and take him out with us.' Darnel turned to Tomaz. 'Can you get into the security hut? Return his radio and sign him out... Tomaz, can you do it?' Darnel said, raising his voice.

'Err, I... I. Yes, if I can get the guard out of the hut. Yes.'

Minutes later, the body was in the box. Darnel handed Kevin's radio and pass to Tomaz, along with a mobile phone.

'Remember, make the call when the president and prime minister enter the room. Then get out of the building. You've got five minutes before the device goes off. The nerve agent will kill everyone in that room—probably the whole building—in minutes.'

They rattled back through the building the way they'd come until they got to the van. Nobody paid them much attention as they loaded up and signed out. Omar's head bobbed out of sight for a minute then popped back up. He started the van and moved it up to the exit barrier. The engine suddenly died. He turned it over several times, but it refused to fire up. Spencer and Darnel got out and lifted the bonnet up.

'Try it again,' Darnel said.

The engine turned over with no success.

'What's up?' said the security guard, wandering over from the security hut.

'It just died, mate,' said Darnel, looking over the guard's shoulder as Tomaz darted into the hut.

'Omar, try it again, mate,' he yelled.

'Do you wanna call a breakdown truck? You can't leave it here. It's a security risk.'

Darnel saw Tomaz over the guard's shoulder leaving the hut. He gave Darnel a small nod.

'Give it one last try, Omar,' said Darnel, banging twice on the front of the van.

Omar twisted two bare ends of the ignition wire back together and turned the key. The van fired up and roared as Omar pumped the accelerator a few times. Spencer and Darnel slammed the bonnet shut. The guard returned to his hut and opened the barrier. They smiled and waved as he let them through.

———

Inside the building, Tomaz stood shaking slightly as he stared at the mobile phone Darnel had given him to trigger the device. He pocketed the phone, telling himself to get a grip. A few more days and he'd be back in Ukraine, a rich man. Thanks to Marcus Tenby, he'd be able to get his son the operation he needed and take care of his family.

CHAPTER 61

It had taken Gaspar under three hours the previous day to get the phone and broadband information on Tenby's property. It took a frustrated Danny some time longer to get hold of Scott.

'Danny, old man, do you know what time it is?' said a slightly slurry Scott.

'I've been trying to get hold of you for hours.'

'Oh, sorry I've been, err, entertaining. Hang on a sec.'

In the background, Danny could hear a female voice asking Scott to come back to bed.

Despite his frustration, the eavesdropping put a smile on Danny's face.

'Sorry, Danny, what's up?' said Scott.

'What's up, indeed? Who's the lady friend?' Danny said.

'A rather lovely brunette—a receptionist from Leamings—and I'd rather like to get back to her, old boy. So, if you could get to the reason for your call...'

'Right, sorry, yes. We're on the trail of Marcus Tenby and I believe he's here, calling himself Toby Birbeck. I have his phone and broadband details and need you to hack his CCTV. We have to get a positive ID before we can go in.'

'Hmm, hack the hacker's CCTV. I like the sound of that,' said Scott, suddenly turning away from the phone. The line became muffled as he shouted, 'Crystal, darling, you'll have to get dressed. Sorry, my dear. I've got work to do. I'll call you a cab.' Then he was back. 'Send me the details. I'll get straight on it.'

Danny could hear the excitement in his voice.

'Thanks, Scotty. You're the best.'

'I know. I'll call you as soon as I have something.'

Scott hung up. Danny couldn't settle and spent the next few hours pacing around the villa like an expectant father.

At midnight—4.00 a.m. UK time—his phone rang. He snatched it off the arm of the chair.

'Scotty,' he said, anxiously.

'Danny, old man, sorry for the delay. Unsurprisingly, there was more than the usual security to get past. I've got access to his camera system and just emailed you three positive stills identifying this Toby Birbeck as Marcus Tenby. No doubt,' said Scott and yawned into the phone.

'Brilliant, great work. You get some rest,' said Danny.

'Hold your horses, that's not all. Check your email. I've added a second administrator's access account to the CCTV system. Use the online details in the email and you can see all the camera feeds yourself in real time. Plus, you can access all recorded data.'

Danny detected just a little smugness in his voice.

'Top man. I could kiss you,' said Danny, already on his way to Paul's laptop.

'As attractive as that sounds, I think I'll pass. There are three computers on Tenby's network. One's a crappy laptop that the security team uses for emails, schedules and late-night porn. I got into that in minutes. I'll send you copies of anything helpful. The other two must be Tenby's. Very high security, very high spec. It's going to take me a while to get in and I need a few hours' sleep,' said Scott, yawning again.

'That's great. You get some sleep. I'm going to check out the cameras before I get some shut-eye myself. I'll catch up with you in the morning. That's err, your lunchtime, okay?'

'Okay, I'll talk to you later.'

Danny looked at the stills. Sure enough, there was Tenby, large as life.

Paul and Tom had wandered in from the kitchen, curious what had caused the excitement in Danny's voice.

Danny turned the laptop towards them.

'Shit, how the—? Scott, right?' said Tom.

'Right,' said Danny.

He followed Scott's instructions and logged into the camera system, bringing up a grid with eight live feeds from the house.

'Scott Miller. That man's a bloody genius,' said Paul. Crystal-clear images of the security guards doing their rounds filled the screen. The last camera in the grid covered the area just inside the main door.

'That's great. I should be able to work out the guards' schedules from this,' said Tom, leaning in.

'Don't have to. Scott's hacked the security guard's computer. He's got emails, schedules, the lot. He'll send them over in the morning,' said Danny, grinning.

'Let's get some sleep, guys. We'll work out an extraction plan in the morning,' said Paul, patting Danny on the back.

Resigning himself to the tiredness creeping through his body, Danny nodded and logged off.

He turned to Paul.

'I've gotta get this bastard bagged and tagged back to the States. He's got to pay for all those poor sods he's killed.'

Paul nodded. 'Get some rest. Tenby is going nowhere.'

Danny walked into his bedroom and sent Trisha a message: *Miss you. Be home soon.* Then he stripped off and slid into bed. He was asleep within minutes.

CHAPTER 62

The staff canteen sat off the former servants' corridor next to the kitchens at the back of the Foreign Office. Tomaz took a seat in the corner, shoulders hunched, dark rings under his eyes. He drank his second cup of coffee, willing the time away until he could leave. He'd been awake most of the night and his stomach was churning like a washing machine. Every time he closed his eyes, he saw Kevin Trimble's face frozen in horror as Darnel's screwdriver drove up under his chin. He reminded himself why he was doing this. The money from it would pay for his son's heart operation back home. Immigration had refused his entry, meaning the NHS was a no-go. He'd appealed but had failed to get the decision overturned.

'Tomaz, is Douglas McKenna back yet?'

Bill Saunders, head of security, snapped Tomaz away from his thoughts.

'No, he's still off. Sickness bug, I think. Can I help?' he said, trying to hide his nerves.

'Just reminding everyone to make sure all security logs

227

are up to date. We've got security services in later for sweeps and checks for the state visit.' 'Thanks, Bill. Will do.'

At the door, Bill paused and turned back to face Tomaz.

'Did you see Kevin Trimble yesterday afternoon?'

Tomaz's stomach did somersaults. It took all his control not throw up on the spot.

'Hmm, I saw him at lunchtime, I think. He rushed past me. He was on the phone, saying something about being on his way.' Tomaz's legs shook under the table. 'Don't know where. Why?'

'He signed out early yesterday and nobody remembers seeing him leave. He never went home. His wife called us late last night in a terrible state, and the police are out looking for him,' said Bill, looking at this watch.

'Oh no. I hope nothing happened to him on the way home,' said Tomaz.

'Yes, absolutely' came Bill's reply as he headed off down the corridor.

Tomaz sat alone once more. He put his hand in his pocket and ran his fingers across the phone that Darnel had given him. Outside, in the boot of his car, a small suitcase was ready, packed with a passport and ticket under a new identity that Marcus had arranged two months earlier.

———

At 1.00 p.m., two Range Rovers with blacked-out windows entered the service courtyard of the Foreign Office. Edward Jenkins and Glen Silverman climbed out of one. Two unmarked white Transit vans parked next to them. Security personnel in plain black overalls exited the vans and retrieved their excited sniffer dogs from the back.

Edward handed out copies of the schedule for the security sweep. There was no excitement, just a professional calm. They'd been through the procedure dozens of times for countless visiting dignitaries and parliamentary press conferences. Edward and Glen followed Bill into the security hut.

'What can you tell me about M&K Air Conditioning and Heating, Mr Saunders?' said Edward, pointing to the entry in the logbook.

'They were called in by Tomaz Grinzski. He's the maintenance supervisor. There was a fault with the heating in the Grand Reception Room,' said Bill.

'Hmm. I see they were on escorted access, and not security-cleared contractors. Do you not have a heating contractor with clearance?' said Edward.

'Well, Douglas McKenna, the maintenance manager, is off sick. He usually uses Heatsafe when there's a problem. Tomaz said they went under, so he had to call a local company to get it sorted before the visit.'

'Okay, good. They were escorted at all times?' said Edward.

'Yes, Tomaz escorted them himself,' said Bill.

Edward closed the logbook. 'Thank you, Bill. Anything else unusual?'

'Not on site, but a member of staff's been reported missing,' said Bill.

'Kevin Trimble is one of our security team. He signed out and never arrived home. His wife called the police but there's no sign of him.'

'I'll check with the police and see if anything's turned up,' said Edward.

'Thank you, Mr Saunders. You can carry on now.'

The sweep lasted three hours. They discovered no concealed extremists waiting to attack the president or prime minister. The dogs found no trace of explosives. And there were no lines of sight for sniper shots into the Grand Reception Room. The missing guard and a new contractor had bothered Edward, but he was forced to accept that the building was clear. As they prepared to leave, a six-strong team of secret-service agents arrived. They'd make sure no one without clearance or invitation would get in or out of the building between now and the press conference. Edward got in the Range Rover and Glen drove him back to headquarters. Edward tapped a number into his phone.

'Hi, Stew. It's Edward Jenkins. How's life at Scotland Yard? Good, good. I need to know everything you've got on a missing person. A security guard at the Foreign Office. Kevin Trimble left work and never made it home... Thank you, Stew. Just email it to me.'

Edward hung up and rubbed his eyes.

'You okay, boss?' said Glen.

'Coincidences, Glen. I don't like coincidences.'

CHAPTER 63

The sound of raised voices woke Danny up. He'd had a good night's sleep and felt better than he had in days. In the dining room, Lucas and Gaspar were locked in a heated discussion of fast- flowing Spanish.

'Morning, Danny,' said Paul, looking up from the laptop with Tenby's camera feeds.

'Morning, Paul. You been there all night, mate?' Danny said.

'Just a couple of hours. Tom was here since sun-up. He's gone to get his head down for a bit,' Paul said.

'What's up with them two?' said Danny.

'Gaspar thinks we need to abort the mission because Tenby has too many armed security staff,' said Paul, rolling his eyes.

Danny read Tom and Paul's notes and ran through the recorded camera feeds. 'What do you reckon, mate?' said John over Danny's shoulder.

'Hmm, we'll have to go in at night. There are only four

guys on security after 8.00 p.m. One on the gate, two inside the wall on patrol and one in the guardroom.'

'Any idea on how to proceed? They're armed, remember,' said John.

'Lucas and Gaspar can run a little distraction at the gate. You be ready in the car while me and Tom go over the wall at the east corner. Paul will monitor cameras and freeze the image on the corner one before we go over. We'll take out the guards at the wall and in the guard hut, gag and zip-tie 'em, find Tenby and get out the way we came in. In and out, ten minutes tops,' Danny said with a grin.

'That's the Danny, I know,' said Paul. 'When do you want to go?'

'Early hours, say 4.00 a.m. The guards will be bored and tired. Now, what's for breakfast?' said Danny as he jotted down what Gaspar needed to get for the job.

'That's it?' said John, bewildered.

'The simpler the plan the better, mate,' said Danny, chuckling.

'Don't worry. He's always like that. Trust me—there's no one else I'd rather have on this. Now, as the man said, what's for breakfast?' said Paul.

The sun streamed in through the half-open blinds, cutting dusty beams of light across the office. Two laptops sat open. Marcus read the news on one and browsed stocks and shares on the other. He closed the news window and signed into the encrypted-message program. An incoming message from Darnel read: *All is ready. Tomorrow we show the world they will never defeat us. Allah be with Tomaz. It is down to him now. Thank you for the money, brother. As planned, we have split up and will use it to disappear until we are needed again.* Showing no emotion, Marcus closed the message and typed: *Hold your nerve, my friend. In one more day, you and your family will be together. Succeed and your son will get the surgery he so badly needs. Remember, these people wouldn't help you in your time of need. When it's done, I will send you your money. Marcus.*

He sent the message to Tomaz and sat back. For a fraction of a second, the screen flickered. He stared at it for a while, but it didn't happen again, and he glanced back at his shares. Miguel called from the hall.

Perhaps it had been a power surge. He got up and left the room.

Seven thousand miles away, in his modern home office overlooking the Thames, Scott smiled smugly as he began rooting through Tenby's laptop files.

'The dog's bollocks, old boy, if I say so myself. Now, what have you been up to?'

There were two encrypted folders, one named *CY17*. Curiosity piqued, he started the laborious task of cracking them open.

233

CHAPTER 64

The evening ticked by slowly as Danny and the team waited for the early hours. Paul had persuaded Gaspar not to worry about the armed guards and Danny had sent him out with a shopping list. He'd reappeared later that afternoon with every item. Tom and Danny had spent a couple of hours scouring satellite pictures of the house, running through alternative scenarios and checking the radios and tranquilliser dart guns. Tom had been instantly up for the mission. He and Danny were the only two with mission experience and both enjoyed the adrenaline-fuelled excitement reminiscent of their days in the service. They were dressed in black. Knitted black hats that rolled down into balaclavas sat on the table in front of them. To the side lay two Glock 19s. Patches of silver glinted in the dining-room light where the serial numbers had been machined off. Danny picked one up and slid the magazine out. He checked the equipment, then reloaded and placed it in his shoulder holster.

'Only if absolutely necessary, right?' said Tom.

'Right.'

Two telescopic ladders leaned against the wall. They'd use them to get in and back over the property with an unconscious Tenby slung over one of their shoulders. A mobile rang in the kitchen. Two minutes later Paul stormed into the dining room, calling Lucas and John to join him.

He placed his mobile on the table and turned on the speaker. 'Good evening, gentlemen. This is Edward Jenkins. We have a situation of the highest priority to discuss with you. Scott Miller has hacked and decoded files on Marcus Tenby's laptops. They include plans for a dirty bomb that uses a highly toxic nerve gas. Tomorrow's date is referenced, as are the initials *NY*, which we're assuming is New York. Scott, the FBI and MI6 are working flat out to decode the remaining files, but time is short. I have just had an emergency conference call with the prime minister and the president. We need to discuss a plan of action with you.'

'You need us to get the information out of Tenby tonight,' said Danny.

'Well, yes,' replied Edward.

Danny's face was like granite. 'By any means.'

'By any means,' said Edward.

The team nodded at each other.

'Understood. We'll keep you posted.' Danny hung up. 'Okay, same plan only we can't tranq Tenby. It'd take too long for him to come round. We'll gag him and zip-tie his hands and feet, then bring him here for interrogation.'

Danny looked at Paul, who nodded again. Back when he was in intelligence, interrogation had been one of Paul's specialities.

'We all know the drill. Let's get it together.'

CHAPTER 65

omaz sat in the gloom of his rented one-bedroom flat just a short Tube ride from the Foreign Office. He swigged from a bottle of Jack Daniel's. He'd not slept for days. Every time he shut his eyes, Kevin Trimble and the screwdriver attack haunted him. The acid in his stomach was killing him and his hands trembled with the thought of what he had to do. He'd been all set to back out and tip off the security services. That all changed when he'd called his wife. His son's condition was worsening.

He had no choice. Without Marcus's money, his son would be dead in a matter of weeks. He thumbed the passport Marcus had sent him and picked up the airline ticket in the name of Nikali Yentski. He dropped them on top of his packed suitcase and took another big swig before sobbing uncontrollably. At 12.30 p.m. it would be all over. He might burn in hell for eternity, but if his son lived and his family were secure, it was a burden he was prepared to live with.

CHAPTER 66

n the early hours of the morning, John drove the drab Nissan through the empty streets. He approached the ranch house from the rear and headed towards the east corner. Danny and Tom sat in the back, barely visible in the shadows.

'Kill the lights, John,' said Danny when they were within a hundred metres of the wall.

'Mic test, Paul.'

'Check.'

'Gaspar.'

'I hear you.'

'You two all good?' said Danny to Tom and John.

'Yep, all good,' said Tom.

John killed the engine. 'All good.'

'Paul, get ready to put cameras on playback from thirty minutes ago.'

Danny and Tom got out of the car. The street was dark by the wall, the nearest street light over forty metres away. They removed the telescopic ladders from the boot. Tom extended one and rested it against the wall.

'Paul, cameras,' whispered Danny. He rolled the bala-clava down, climbed the ladder, and peeped over the top.

'Roger that. Camera feed playing. You're good to go,' said Paul in his ear.

The lights from the house weren't bright enough to cut through the darkness surrounding the landscaped borders by the wall. Danny waited for his eyes to acclimatise to the dark. He spotted the guard walking towards the front of the wall. The man's back was to him. He nimbly swung his legs over and dropped into a squat behind the bushes and shrubs.

'Clear. Pass the ladder down, Tom.'

Tom did as instructed, then dropped into position beside Danny. They watched through the foliage as the guard turned around to walk back towards them.

'Gaspar, on my mark, drive up to the front gate and tranq the guard.'

'Okay.'

The wall guard shuffled towards the rear of the garden. His sub-machine gun swung casually under his arm on its shoulder strap. He tapped on his phone with his thumbs. A hand clamped over his mouth and dart went into his neck. He looked up, confused and frightened. Within seconds, the drug had spirited him away. Tom pushed him back-wards. Danny caught him and dragged him into the cover of the foliage.

'Take out the guard at the gate, Gaspar,' Danny said.

Gaspar's confirmation crackled over the mic.

Danny waved a command to Tom, and they moved stealth-like towards a door at the rear of the house. A loud crackle over the headset caused Danny and Tom to bob down against the wall by the back door.

'Sound off,' whispered Danny.

'Check,' said Paul.

'Check,' said John.

'Check,' said Tom beside him.

'Gaspar,' said Danny, 'Sound off.'

'Paul, as soon as I take out the guard in the control room, bring the cameras up and check on Gaspar. His mic's out.'

'Will do.'

Danny set his back flat against the wall then swung around to glance through the window. The hall was clear. He tried the door—it was unlocked. He looked around again. Satisfied all was quiet, he gestured for them to move into the house. They followed the floor plan memorised from the estate agent's advertisement and moved silently towards the control room. The door was slightly ajar. Tom moved to open it further. Danny raised the tranquilliser gun with one hand and did a three-finger countdown with the other. One—Tom threw open the door and Danny swept in. The guard was slumped over the desk in a pool of blood. Someone had cut his throat from ear to ear.

'Paul, we've got a dead security guard. Cameras up, check on Gaspar.'

'They're all down, Danny. Get out.'

Danny looked at Tom, who nodded.

'Can't do that. We've gotta find out where that bomb is,' he whispered.

They exited the control room, swept through the two rooms next door, then peeped into the main lounge. Two young Arabic men with dark, long hair and beards stood armed with AK-47 assault rifles. Danny's hand signalled 'eyes on two' and 'split location', then holstered his gun and pulled out a large commando knife. Tom nodded and did the same, then tucked up close beside him. One man had his back to them. The other was looking at his phone. Danny tensed and waited for the second man to turn around. Screams and groans echoed from the back of the house. The men spoke in Arabic and turned towards the noise. Danny and Tom sprang into the lounge, reaching the men in unison. They clamped their mouths and drove the knives into the base of their skulls, killing them instantly. They held them firmly and let the bodies slide quietly to the floor. Knives sheathed, they drew their guns and headed towards the source of the screams. They stopped outside Tenby's office, one either side of the frame, listening. There were three men in the room.

'Again' came a deep, gruff voice. A thud followed, then more groaning.

'No, Hassan, you've got it wrong. It was Barzan and Kadah who killed Akbar. I killed them to avenge your brother.'

It was Tenby's pained voice.

Hassan's voice sounded close to the door. Tenby's was harder to hear so further away. He tried to gauge the position of the third man.

'I don't believe you, you lying dog. This is for my brother. You will burn in the depths of hell!'

Danny threw open the door. It knocked Hassan off his feet. The gun went off as Hassan fell, the sound deafening in the small room. Tom dived behind Danny and hit the wall off-balance, landing with his gun extended and eyes locked on. He let off two shots at the man standing beside Tenby's bloodied kneeling body. The bullets struck him in the centre of his chest and knocked him backwards. Hassan, still on the floor, swung his gun back up and Danny put three shots into him. Time froze as the gun smoke cleared and the ringing in his ears subsided. Tenby slowly raised his head and looked straight at Danny, his eyes burning with fury. But only briefly. Blood streamed from the bullet hole in his chest.

'Shit, no, no, no.'

Danny lay Tenby down and applied pressure on the wound.

'Paul, opposition eliminated, but the target is down. John, drive past the front and look for Gaspar and Lucas. Eyes open for hostiles. We'll evac front gate.'

'Roger,' said Paul.

'Roger that,' said John.

Tenby's eyes rolled in his head and his breathing was laboured. Tom took over putting pressure on the wound while Danny slapped Tenby hard to focus him.

'Marcus, listen to me. Where in New York is the bomb?' he yelled.

'New Yo... Nikali Yen... ha, you fools,' said Tenby, sneering through his blooded mouth.

A gunshot came from outside.

'John, come in,' said Tom.

Silence.

'John, come in' repeated Tom.

Silence.

'Hostile down. Gaspar and Lucas are dead. Gate's open, car's ready. Get a move on. I can hear sirens in the distance,' said John.

'Where's the bomb, you bastard?' Danny grabbed Tenby's hair, forcing him to look him in the eyes.

Tenby spat bloody globules. 'You're too late. Your leaders are dead.'

Danny pulled his knife from its sheath and jammed it hard into Tenby's thigh, driving it down to the bone. Coughing out blood as he screamed, Tenby arched his back.

'Where is the bomb?' Danny said, twisting the knife.

Tom looked at Danny and shook his head. Blood

continued to spill from the bullet wound despite his attempts to stem the flow.

'You're too late,' Tenby spat weakly.

'You've gotta move, guys. Time's short,' said John over the headset.

Danny twisted the knife once more.

'Tomaz,' he said, and his body went limp.

'Fuck, fuck!' said Danny. 'Grab those laptops and let's go.'

Tom and Danny ran through the house and out the gate.

'Tom, drive Gaspar's car. Danny, jump in here. Come on, guys—we've gotta go. Now!'

The flashing blue lights closed in on the villa as they sped off down the dark side road and back to base.

CHAPTER 67

Tom pulled into the large double garage and glanced at Lucas and Gaspar's bodies. He closed the door behind him to keep the car out of sight and walked with Danny and John into the villa. In the dining room, Paul nodded as he talked on the phone. Sheets of paper lay in front of him, arrows pointing to scribbles as he tried to link all the data.

'Yes, Patrick,' he said. 'We tracked and arrested the fixer in London prior to coming to New York. He was supplying ID to Tenby and had a driving licence at his property in the name of Nikali Yentski. The point is, the bomb isn't in New York. NY is for Nikali Yentski. Before he died Tenby said, "Your leaders are dead," and one name— Tomaz— which means nothing to me.'

Paul waited for Patrick Fallen's response.

'My God. Get hold of Jenkins, NOW. He's at a press conference with the prime minister and the president in London. I'll try to warn the president's security detail. Sit tight. I'll call you as soon as they're safe.'

Paul speed-dialled Edward.

'Jenkins.'

'It's Paul. The bomb is there with you. You've got to evacuate before it's activated. We've got two names—Nikali Yentski from a fake driving licence made by Hamish Cambell, and a first name of Tomaz.'

'Got it.'

Edward hung up and worked his way across the back of the Grand Reception Room. At the front, the prime minister and president were shaking hands and taking their places at the podiums. Avoiding panic was essential. He walked around the room towards the secret-service agents who'd initiate an evacuation protocol. Nikali Yentski meant nothing to him but the name Tomaz niggled. He got to the back corner of the room as a member of Foreign Office staff passed him and exited through the rear doors. His movements were a little too urgent. Edward was sure he'd seen him before. He stopped mid-step.

Tomaz Grinzski.

He turned and sprinted out the room, diving towards Tomaz as he reached the stairs.

'Tomaz Grinzski, you're under arrest. Where is the bomb?' Edward twisted Tomaz's arm into a lock.

'It's too late! You have to let me go. We have to go,' said Tomaz, his eyes wide with panic.

Glen Silverman appeared next to them and grabbed Tomaz, cuffing him as Edward sounded the alarm over the radio.

'Code red, code red, code red.'

Secret-service agents flew into action, leading the prime minister and president away down the back corridors.

'Where's the bomb?' said Edward, his face close to Tomaz's.

Glen hoisted him to his feet and slammed him back against the wall.

'There's no time. We've got to get out. We'll all die. It's in the plant room over there.'

Tomaz sobbed. Edward and Glen dragged him past the packed Grand Reception Room and into the plant room. '*Where?*'

'Up there behind the ducting flap. There's no time. We have to get out. I'm sorry. I didn't want to do it. I'm sorry.'

Glen grabbed the stepladder and Edward shot up and spun the wing nuts. He peered into the duct and reached in. His hand found something and he pulled.

Two yellow cylinders were handed carefully down to Glen. A small digital clock next to a mobile phone was counting down... thirty-seven, thirty-six, thirty-five.

'Can you stop it?' Edward said, pulling out a small set of scissors from his penknife.

Thirty, twenty-nine, twenty-eight...

'Give me some light with your phone,' said Glen as he eased the clock forward, exposing four wires.

Twenty-three, twenty-two, twenty-one...

Edward illuminated the device as Glen traced the wires. Sweat trickled down their faces.

Seventeen, sixteen, fifteen...

'Glen,' said Edward, eyeing the timer.

'I know, I know,' said Glen. The tiny scissors shook in his hand as he hovered over the blue wire.

Ten, nine, eight...

Glen squeezed gently.

Five, four, three...

The blue plastic sheath separated.

Glen shook his head. Moving across, he snipped the green wire.

They crouched next to the device, hearts racing.

The longest seconds of their lives followed before it sunk in. They had disarmed the bomb.

Edward reached for his radio. 'This is Tango One Two. We need a full evac and containment team. Call in the regiment—chemical and biological. ASAP. Over.'

'Roger that. What is your location and situation? Over.' It was the voice of Edward's commander-in-chief.

'First-floor plant room off the Grand Reception Room landing. We have a device disarmed and one suspect apprehended.'

Edward sat back against the wall and let out a long sigh.

Tomaz Grinzski sank to his knees. Tears rolled down his cheeks. 'I'm sorry, so sorry. My son, my wife. Forgive me.'

CHAPTER 68

The mood in the villa was sombre, and the wait had everyone's nerves on edge. After a tense couple of hours, Patrick Fallen called Paul back.

'Great job, guys. Everyone's safe and the bomb has been disarmed. Sit tight. We're putting a plan together to get you, the laptops and the bodies of Gaspar and Lucas Stateside. I've been told to ask you to put everything you used in bin bags and leave them there. Then shower, change and pack, and be ready to go. There'll be a clean-up crew coming in after we pick you up. On behalf of the United States of America, the president thanks you.' Forty minutes later, they sat around the dining-room table with four glasses and a bottle of La Alazana whiskey. Paul poured a shot for each of them.

'Lucas and Gaspar,' he said.

They raised their glasses and drank to fallen friends.

As the sun began to set, two large FedEx vans turned up. Undercover FBI agents issued them with FedEx uniforms and security passes, then headed for the garage for the bodies of Lucas and Gaspar. The clean-up team remained outside until they left for the FedEx World Service Centre at Ezeiza Airport. They followed the agents into the freight terminal and passed through a security checkpoint where the staff were only marginally interested in them.

Less than an hour later, they were en route to New York.

CHAPTER 69

anny's pocket vibrated with the steady rhythm of an incoming call. He pulled out his phone and smiled.

'Yo, little bruv. I'm just about to get a taxi to yours.'

'Na, don't do that. Me and Scott are pulling into the pickup bay now,' said Rob. Danny was about to ask what they were driving when a throaty exhaust and thumping music coming from a Jaguar F-Pace SVR gave the game away. A grinning Rob climbed out of the front and the two brothers hugged.

'Get a room, you tarts,' said Scott, turning the music down.

Same old, same old.

'Scotty boy, you're looking better, mate,' said Danny, noticing the plaster cast still on Scott's leg.

Scott tapped the cast. 'It comes off next week. Lucky it's my left leg. I can still drive an automatic.'

He powered the V8 engine out of the pickup zone and onto the exit road.

'So, old man, don't keep us in suspense. Let's have a peep,' said Scott.

Danny rolled his eyes and fished a red leather box from the pouch on his rucksack.

'Satisfied?' he said.

Scott whistled and Rob patted his brother on the back.

'The Presidential Medal of Freedom. Very impressive. All I got was a lousy six million dollars for my software. It's just so unfair,' said Scott with a chuckle.

Danny laughed.

'You're such an arsehole!'

'Jokes aside. What are you going to do now you're back?' said Rob.

'Well, although I'm not in the league of this idiot, thanks to Paul I got paid very handsomely from both MI6 and the United States government. So, I'm going house-hunting,' said Danny.

'So, you're not going away again?'

'No, Rob, I'm not going away, and I'll be here for your wedding. Paul's offered me a permanent position as security director, so I'm back to stay.'

An hour later they pulled up at the old Georgian four-bedroom semi that always transported him back to his childhood. Sitting on the drive was a brand-new top-of-the-line blue BMW M4.

'Whose is the flash motor?' said Danny.

Scott turned to face him and pulled a set of keys from his pocket.

'I rather think it's yours, old boy.'

'What? Scott, no, I can't take that.'

'Yes, you can. Just think of it as a commission for getting me in with the banks,' said Scott, thrusting the keys in Danny's hand.

'Now bugger off. I've got a date with a certain young brunette.'

Danny and Rob grinned and waved him off.

Laughter and the smell of good home-cooked food drifted from the kitchen. Rob patted Tina on the bum as she cooked over the stove. Danny walked in to Trisha's warm smile.

'Hello, you,' Danny said.

'Hello, you,' she said, and pulled him towards her.

CHAPTER 70

Over the week that followed, Scott helped MI6 decipher the data on Tenby's laptops. Once they'd added the information Hamish Cambell had given up, the arrests started. They picked Darnel up at Heathrow as he checked in for a flight to Johannesburg with a false passport. Omar was arrested as he tried to board a flight from Stansted to Amsterdam. Spencer was cornered in Dover's ferry terminal. He pulled a gun and was shot dead by armed police. Scott worked his magic and tracked the stolen money, returning everything that Tenby hadn't already spent. For a small reward, of course. Edward and Patrick used the full resources of the FBI and MI6 to track down the CY17 supplier and former KGB agent, Rufus Petrov, to the island of Crete. Petrov had overseen the destruction of chemical weapons at the end of the Cold War but had smuggled several crates out and been selling them on the black market ever since. Interpol had detained Petrov, who was now in a Greek holding cell, awaiting questioning.

CHAPTER 71

Danny house-hunted and treated Scott to the various pub lunches he owed him, while spending his evenings with Trisha. His aches and pains soon went, and he decided it was time to get back in the gym. There was only one option: Pullman's. Big Dave had bought the rundown gym after leaving the army twenty years earlier, and he'd built it up into a successful business with all the latest equipment. Danny pushed through the squeaky gym doors at 7.30 a.m.

'Danny,' Dave said casually without looking up from the reception desk.

'Dave,' Danny replied, enjoying the ritual greeting.

'You back for long?' Dave said, slowly lifting his head to look Danny square in the eyes.

'So, it would seem.'

'You better fuck off and do some training then. You look soft as shit.' Dave dismissed him with a wave of his hand.

Danny chuckled. 'Yes, sir.'

The gym was empty apart from a young Lycra-clad woman standing on one of the running machines. She selected a playlist on her phone and nodded her head in time to the music, then fired up a treadmill. As she jogged, her blonde ponytail swished from side to side. Danny started to bench press, enjoying the feeling of muscle against metal as he added more weights to his workout.

———

The door squeaked open and a large man in baggy hoody entered reception. A baseball cap with its peak pulled low covered his eyes.

'Morning. You're not a member, would you like to join, or would you like to pay as a guest?' Dave said, looking up from the PC.

The man tilted his head, displaying the blistered skin covering the left-hand side of his face. He grinned from ear to ear.

'Yeah, a guest. That'd be nice.' His head tilted again, revealing intense blue eyes. Dave remained motionless for a second, momentarily unnerved.

'How much?' the guy said.

'Five pounds, please. And you need to fill in a guest form,' Dave said, passing over a clipboard.

The man's arm whipped up and a massive knuckle-dusted fist crashed into Dave's head like a steam train. Dave flew from his seat into the shelf behind. Tubs of protein powder and energy bars crashed around him. The man walked calmly behind the desk and reached up to the CCTV, switching it off. Dave tried to get up but the man rained more blows into his jaw and nose. The guy stared, breathing heavily, then walked over to the door, dropped the lock, and flipped the *Closed* sign around. The guy tipped his cap back and headed into the gym.

——————

Danny had worked his way up to 110 kilograms. Now he sat looking forward while he caught his breath. On the far wall beside the squat rack was a window that looked through to reception. The tubs, snacks and drinks on the shelves were in disarray, and there was no sign of Dave. The hairs stood up on the back of his neck as his sixth sense tingled. He sensed movement in his peripheral vision. Approaching fast. He hooked his heels into the base of the bench and pushed back hard, sliding himself off the bottom. A cast-iron weight crashed onto the bench edge. It had missed Danny's head by millimetres, splitting instead the vinyl and foam cladding down to the metal frame. Above stood a crazed, scarred face. Snipe. Danny flipped into a forward roll and bumped painfully into a dumbbell rack. He looked back around. Snipe grabbed a long steel bar from one of the lat machines then came at him fast.

'Payback time, Pearson,' he growled.

Every man has a fight-or-flight instinct when his back's against the wall. Danny's was fight. He grabbed a dumb-bell from the rack and launched himself forward as Snipe took a two-handed swing. There was a terrific clang as bar struck dumbbell, rendering them motionless for a split second. First to recover, Danny twisted to one side and gave two quick, powerful kidney blows with his free hand. They should have dropped an elephant, but Snipe just folded to one side slightly before swinging the bar back fast. It caught Danny on one of his shoulders, knocking him over a bench and into a pile of stacked weights. The dumbbell flew out of his hand, clanging loudly against a cross-trainer. Ignoring the pain, he grabbed a steel weight, hurling it like a discus at the approaching Snipe, catching him squarely in the chest. The blow knocked Snipe backwards. The bar flew from his hand as he landed, sprawled between two rowing machines.

Ten feet behind them, the woman continued to jog on the running machine, headphones on, unaware of the chaos behind her. Danny lunged forward, planting a sprinting-kick to Snipe's groin that slid him backwards. He groaned and rolled back between the cycle machines before standing up slightly bent over. His face was a mixture of pain, fury and insanity. With a huge roar, he lifted a cycle machine clean off the ground and threw it at Danny, catching him mid-torso and sending him flying into the dumbbell rack. The unforgiving hunks of metal dug into his back and ribs. Fuelled with adrenaline, Danny grabbed a dumbbell and ran towards a rowing machine. He jumped high off the seat and drove the metal weight hard into his face. Snipe's nose exploded in a fountain of blood as he lurched backwards onto the empty treadmill next to the jogging woman. She looked in shock at Snipe's bloody form. Whipping upright, Snipe shook his head and looked over at her. He grinned and planted a fist into the side of her head, shattering the headphones. She bounced off the side bars of the treadmill like a pinball and lost her footing. Her body hit the base hard, and it catapulted her off the back of the machine into a crumpled heap.

Danny dared not give Snipe the upper hand. He drove another iron-clad punch to his head, but Snipe moved fast, dodged the blow, and delivered an elbow to Danny's ribs. He followed with a blistering combination to the kidneys and ribs. Danny felt the wind rip from his lungs. Snipe picked him up around the middle and charged forward, cracking Danny's head on a bar hanging from a cable of the tall multi-gym. He was dumped onto the machine with a painful crack on the sliding-weight stack. Head spinning, Danny tried to keep his arms raised as Snipe rained punches down on him.

'Ain't fucking golden boy now, are you?'

Forearms up, Danny tried to block.

'Ten fucking years I've been waiting for this,' said Snipe. 'You should have seen your wife and kid's face as I drove the fucking lorry over their car. Fucking classic.'

A numbness washed over Danny as the words hit him. He glanced left and spotted the locking pin in the multi-gym's weight stack. Fury replaced numbness as he yanked out the pin and stabbed it into Snipe's inner thigh.

'Fuck!' Snipe dropped the weight as he screamed and grabbed his thigh. The machine's bar had dropped to the ground when Danny had pulled out the pin. He scooped it up and cracked it over the side of Snipe's head, then spun the cable round his neck and twisted the bar at the back. Snipe clawed wildly at the cable as Danny leapt on top of the weight stack. It yanked Snipe up like a jack-in-the-box as the cable drew back fast into the machine. Danny reached down and shoved the bloody pin back in at the bottom of the stack, engaging all the weights and his body weight to the cable around Snipe's neck. The cable tightened, cutting into Snipe's neck as he danced on tiptoes. His face burned red, veins bulging as he grunted air into his lungs. He twisted around and grabbed the cable above his head. Then, with both feet on the side of the multi-gym, he pushed, lifting Danny and the stack a foot off the ground. The scene stopped as though freeze-framed. Snipe's fury-filled eyes locked on Danny's. His face turned purple and his teeth ground in hate. Danny pushed harder against the top of the machine, forcing the stack back down and the cable to bite ever tighter around Snipe's neck. He watched as the tiny veins in the whites of Snipe's eyes ruptured. Finally, the man-mountain dropped, and his body went limp.

The weights stack clanged to its final resting place and silence filled the room.

CHAPTER 72

He walked slowly through the gated arch of the City of London Cemetery. The lush green of the towering tree canopy stood in sharp contrast to the greys, creams and whites of the gravestones. He reached the familiar headstone with an ornately carved stone cross, then turned and headed along the long row. The bright summer sun and chirping birds tried their best to lift his sombre mood. He faced the two graves he knew so well and crouched. On one he placed a toy car; on the other, a fresh vase of vibrant tiger lilies. Reaching forward, he slipped the blue ribbon over the corner of the headstone. The medal clinked on the hard surface. He stood for a while, deep in his memories, then turned and moved back the way he'd come.

———

A little further down, the groundsman watched him go. His curiosity piqued, he wandered over to look at what the man had hooked on the headstone. He read the inscriptions:

Sarah Ann Pearson Beloved Wife and Mother I'll Love You Forever

Timothy Robert Pearson Beloved Son, I'll Never Forget

Reaching forward he tilted the medal towards him—a frame of golden eagles surrounded a red pentagon with an overlaid white star. In the centre, a blue circle housed thirteen gold stars.

He looked after the man who'd left it, but he was gone.

———

Danny strolled through the gates towards the woman sitting on a bench. She stood as he approached and smiled reassuringly.

'You ok Danny?' she said with a melancholy smile he took her hand. 'Yeah, I'm good. Let's go home.'